The Road To ENGLE BYEN

DAVID GOLDON

Book two in the ENGLE BYEN series

The Road To
Engle Byen

SECOND EDITION
~ January 2019

**Includes the first two chapters of
Book Three in the series**

ENGLE BYEN: OPPORTUNITIES

David Goldon

DAVID GOLDON

Contact: DavidGol**dd**on@gmail.com
www.DavidGoldon.com

Exclusive management, promotion and editing through:
AVA ORION Media
Melbourne, Australia

www.AvaOrionMedia.com

Editor, Proofreader, Formatting &
Design: Michael Young
www.MichaelYoungAuthor.com

DAVID GOLDON

CONTENTS:

DAVID GOLDON

Foreword

One foot after the other, one step at a time, just keep walking. The path to your dreams will reveal itself as you open up your heart.

There was a time when ENGLE BYEN didn't exist. Then, a second later, it was as if it had always been there. That is the power of creativity.

For so many years I have been in awe of my favourite songwriters and performers, like ABBA and Kate Bush, as they have delivered to us so many gifts of classic musical art. They work their magic to capture clouds of inspiration blowing in the breeze then turn them into something real that can move us and change us. They have a divine gift that they've learned to share with us.

Writing stories is precisely the same mysterious alchemy. DAVID GOLDON also has that magical gift. He only needed to realise it, begin to open his heart and live in it.

The world of ENGLE BYEN is populated by amazing people, as real as you and I. They're only a breath away from our reality. Every time we are given a glimpse through the mirror into their world is an exciting and moving adventure for us.

As we publish **THE ROAD TO ENGLE BYEN** for the second time, David is writing book four in the ENGLE BYEN series, and they just keep getting better! I am honoured to be a part of the process that brings the magic of ENGLE BYEN to the world.

One day soon, this book and others will be filmed. I'm determined to see that happen because the world needs to experience the beauty and magic of the world DAVID GOLDON has created ... the road to ENGLE BYEN leads far beyond here... to a place of creativity beyond even our wildest dreams.

Thank you for sharing the journey with us!

MICHAEL YOUNG
January 2019

AVA ORION Media

www.AvaOrionMedia.com

www.MichaelYoungAuthor.com

MichaelYoung3030@gmail.com

DAVID GOLDON

The Road To
Engle Byen

DAVID GOLDON

Book two in the ENGLE BYEN series

DAVID GOLDON

Dedication

This book is dedicated to the tiny angels that whisper ideas and words into my ear.

Also, to my three other "angels" at home...
Michael, Merlin & Millie.

DAVID GOLDON

CHAPTER ONE:
The Club

"You're an angel," the slightly plump Madonna impersonator lip-synced while looking into Michael's ice blue eyes. Embarrassed by the attention, Michael looked away breaking eye contact with the drag queen.

At almost six-foot, high cheekbones, chiselled jaw and a well-toned muscular body, Michael had model good looks. He'd often attract the attention of men, women and drag queens as well, wherever he went.

As the music faded and the drag queen left the stage, the *thump, thump* of loud dance music filled the club. The crowd surrounding him began to disperse, many club-goers making their way straight to the bar.

Michael remained standing in the same spot glancing over to the queue at the bar. He waited for it to thin out before heading over for his usual lemon, lime, and bitters.

"Hey, I think Flab-donna has the hots for you, she couldn't keep her eyes off you," came a voice from behind Michael. He turned around to see a short old man smiling at him.

"Yeah, I noticed she kept looking and singing at me, I didn't know where to look," Michael laughed.

"What brings a handsome young man like yourself to a dingy club like this? Are you waiting for your boyfriend to arrive?" the old guy asked.

"I don't have a boyfriend. I just finished work and came here to wind down."

"Sorry, bit hard to hear, you'll have to move in closer. What do you do for a job?"

"I'm a nurse at the hospital not far from here, I often pop into this club for a while, have a drink, a bit of a dance and then go home," Michael replied in the loudest voice he could muster without screaming at the old guy.

"Never alone I'm sure, you're such a gorgeous hunk," the old guy said as he grabbed Michael on the arse and squeezed.

Usually, up for a chat with new people of any age, Michael turned and walked away without saying anything to the old guy. He hates that he can't have a conversation with someone without there being an ulterior motive.

The queue at the bar had thinned, Michael made his way over to it through the crowd of sweaty clubbers. The Muscle Mary behind the bar ignored the other patrons waiting for service and headed straight to Michael.

"What can I get you tonight gorgeous?" The Muscle Mary asked flashing a smile, teeth whiter than the polar ice caps.

Michael's eyes scanned the tattoos on the barman's chest and arms. "Lemon, lime and bitters, thanks."

As the barman turned around to prepare his drink, Michael couldn't help but notice the barman's tight denim shorts and pert bubble butt. Taking a five dollar note out of his wallet, Michael held it out for the barman to take. He squeezed Michael's hand closed, smiled, handed him his drink, and moved on to the next customer.

Standing near the dance floor, drink in hand, Michael admired the muscled torso's dripping in sweat and moving in unison to the beat of the dance music. His favourite dance anthem of all time began to thump out of the speakers. Placing his unfinished drink on the nearby ledge, he moved onto the dance floor and started moving his body to the thumping rhythm. Wide-eyed men stared at him, their hair and faces dripping in sweat.

He felt hands on his hips. His t-shirt moved up his stomach. He raised his arms up in the air allowing his t-shirt to be taken off by a stranger dancing behind him. The stranger tucked Michael's t-shirt into the back of his designer jeans. He turned and smiled at the handsome young stranger, who was also shirtless, and they danced together until the song ended.

Finding himself in the middle of the dance floor covered in sweat and with a dry mouth, he navigated his way through the masses of bodies to get back and finish his drink. He picked up his glass and guzzled the refreshing beverage. He turned away from the dance floor, making his way to the bar, his shoes sticking to the tacky carpet. He needed water and fast.

His legs began to wobble like jelly as the room spun. Fearing he was about to collapse, he looked for somewhere to sit. He spied a vacant barstool against a wall and stumbled towards it. Once seated, he couldn't feel his legs. His arms felt numb and lifeless. The *thump, thump* of the dance music pulsated in his head.

A thick fog of dry ice pumped into the club, the old guy with the roving hands appeared as if by magic right in front of him. He tried to steady himself by leaning against the wall.

"You all right there handsome? You had too much to drink?" The old guy asked as he rubbed Michael's leg with his wrinkled old hand.

Michael tried to speak but was unable. His limbs became flaccid, his heart began racing; he knew he had been drugged. The old guy put his hand around the back of Michael's neck massaging it.

"Let's get you home. I'll take good care of you."

"Fuck off, you dirty old letch!" came a loud voice out of nowhere. The old man released his grip on Michael and went tumbling back against the wall, sliding down it and landing on the sticky carpet. Almost incapacitated and unable to speak, Michael grinned at the guy who assaulted the old guy. Out of the blue two big burly bouncers pushed their way through the crowd over to him after witnessing the violent confrontation unfold.

"Are you with him?" one of the bouncers asked the violent hero.

"Yeah, I am, this old guy was sleazing onto my boyfriend and wouldn't take no for an answer. Sorry, but I had to do something to stop him."

"Yeah, well you and your boyfriend, who's not looking so good, better leave now." The other bouncer helped the old guy up from the floor, sitting him down on a nearby barstool.

The violent hero took Michael's t-shirt out from the back of his jeans and put it back on him. The bouncer assisted lifting Michael off the barstool and escorted him out to the front of the club with help from the violent hero.

CHAPTER TWO:
The Rude Awakening

A bright light was shining on Michael's face as he opened his eyes. The brightness was too much. He turned away from the light realising it was the sun shining through a window.

Disorientated, he saw a digital clock on a bedside table; the time was 12:34 pm. He looked up at the unfamiliar dirty ceiling and surveyed his surrounds.

There was a computer desk, a rack of CD's, an old chest of drawers and some framed prints on the wall; all cheap and nasty, like you would expect to find in a student's bedroom. He realised he was lying naked on his back in someone else's bed. He turned up his nose at the putrid smell of stale cigarette smoke.

Fragments of what had transpired last night began to flash through his mind. That old man who drugged him and the violent hero that saved him.

Michael sat up in the strange bed amongst unfamiliar surrounds. There was no one else with him in the bed. Sitting on the edge of the bed, he reached over and retrieved his unmistakable garments from the piles of clothes on the floor. As he began to put them on, he noticed some red marks on his wrists, a few bruises on his chest, and his behind was quite painful.

The bedroom door opened taking Michael by surprise. From behind it appeared a plain looking guy with a plump figure, some awful undistinguishable tattoos on his arm. He wore sleep shorts and a white singlet.

"Uh, hi," Michael said. "I guess you were the guy who saved me last night, so thanks, I appreciate it. I think that old guy spiked my drink while I was on the dance floor. He tried to chat me up earlier, and I wasn't interested and..."

"Oh, it wasn't him," the violent hero guy interrupted, "It was me, and you better go get yourself an AIDS test too. Now I have my revenge you can fuck off out of here you psycho nut job."

Dazed and confused; Michael had never met this guy before so what revenge would he be seeking? He dressed quickly. Looking at this disturbed individual standing at the bedroom door, Michael pushed past him not saying a word.

Walking fast-paced along a small hallway, he saw the front door and bolted towards it. His hands trembled as he turned the locks on the door, hoping all the while that psycho hadn't locked him in. Success! The door was unlocked.

Slamming the door shut behind him, he found himself in a stairwell surrounded by other units. It was an older style apartment building which was dark and cold. There was a window in the stairwell from which he could see the street outside. He ran as fast as he could down one flight of stairs. Finding the exit, he flung the door open and leapt over a few steps onto the footpath and the safety of the sunny street.

Relived to be free of that monster, he ran as fast as his designer dress shoes would carry him, which wasn't as fast as he could usually run. The street was narrow, older style apartments lined both sides.

Seeing a small park in the distance, he headed towards it. There were kids on playground equipment. Michael walked towards a tree and sat underneath it to regain his breath. He watched kids playing, his mind drifted, reminiscing about his childhood. His life had changed so much since those early days of innocence.

Snapping back into reality, Michael began to sob uncontrollably as he recalled the situation he had just escaped. Some of the kids in the playground gave him weird looks when they heard him crying.

"Oh shit!" Michael gasped as he felt for his phone. He was relieved to find it was still in his pocket. He stood and took it out. Looking at it, trying to focus, he wiped the tears from his eyes and attempted to regain his composure. It didn't take him long to figure out who he was going to call; his best friend, Dylan.

"Dylan, I've been drugged, kidnapped, tied up, raped and I have AIDS, all a part of someone plotting revenge on me," Michael blurted as soon as Dylan answered his call.

"What Michael? Slow down, you are such a drama queen. Calm down and tell me what's going on."

"Well, I managed to escape, and I just ran and ran, and I'm here in a park, can you come and get me please?"

"Sure, where are you?"

"I don't know, in a park somewhere."

"Michael," Dylan said sternly, "calm down, get yourself together and tell me where you are."

"But I don't know where I am," Michael replied hysterically.

"Okay, you have a navigator app on your phone, turn it on and let me know where you are." His fingers trembled as he located the app on his phone and turned it on. To his surprise, he was in Prahran just one suburb away from his home in South Yarra.

"Dylan, I'm not very far from my place, but you still have to come and pick me up, I need you to examine me."

After Michael had informed Dylan of his location, Dylan immediately left his penthouse apartment located in the heart of Melbourne city.

Dylan is a doctor, at six foot, built like a gladiator he tells anyone who'll listen he's a direct descendant of Scandinavian Vikings, his dance card is always full. Generally, when word gets out he's a natural blond and a doctor, there is a feeding frenzy of people wanting to be his best friend and more.

He was best friends with Michael's identical twin brother, Zac; they met at university where they both studied medicine and graduated together. Michael and Dylan were dating for a while, but it just became too weird for Dylan to be dating someone who looked just like his best friend, who was also like a brother to him, so had to call it off.

Dylan was at his friend's side within ten minutes of his desperate phone call. He drove Michael to his nearby medical practice.

"Michael, you haven't been interfered with, so I doubt you have HIV. We'll do a blood test though and can go from there. The bruising on your wrists indicates you've been restrained in some way. Your drug test shows positive for Rohypnol, which is more commonly referred to as a 'date rape' drug. I'm sure you've have had dealings with it at the hospital. The drug will show up in your blood for about 24 hours. I'm giving you a medical certificate for seven days. It won't be a good look for a nurse to return a positive result if they give you a random drug test at work." Dylan said in his best doctor's voice.

"But Dylan, my bottom is hurting, are you sure I haven't been raped?"

Dylan sighed, "No Michael, you have haemorrhoids." They both laughed hysterically.

"But," Dylan interrupted, "being drugged is quite serious, you should report it to the police."

"Yeah, I guess you are right, but I can't remember where I was, and I don't know if I would recognise him again. He did say something about getting his revenge on me, but I don't know what I've done. I'm sure I haven't laid eyes on him before," bleated Michael.

"Michael, if I am to be truthful with you, Zac did have quite a few enemies out in the club scene. He treated a lot of people quite badly. Perhaps this guy was one of them, and he mistook you for Zac. Perhaps he just wanted to scare you by telling you to get checked for HIV."

"Yeah but Zac has been dead for almost two years now and...."

"Michael, Zac was stabbed to death in a frenzied attack, probably by some drug addict. The crowd he used to run with were a bit suspect, to say the least."

CHAPTER THREE:
The Gardener

Small stones made a crunching noise under the tyres of Michael's car as he drove slowly along the horseshoe-shaped driveway into the front yard of his parents' home in Toorak. He parked his car a short walk from the front door.

As he walked, he admired the well-trimmed dark green hedges and topiaries of various shapes and sizes. Two massive pillars stood at the top of the three steps up to the grand front entrance of the two-storey mansion. He could hear the water feature bubbling away as it cascaded into a pond covered by water lilies and filled with goldfish.

Bob, his parents' long-time gardener, was crouched down trimming the hedges. He was wearing his wide-brimmed hat and sunglasses to protect him from the harsh Australian sun. His uniform consisted of a green polo shirt with the logo 'Bob's Gardening' emblazed in bold yellow letters across the back.

"Hey Bob, how are you doing?" Michael said not caring for or expecting an answer as he walked past Bob and headed to the front door.

Elaine Pridemoore, a former high fashion model, was searching frantically around the house for the keys to her car. She was interrupted by the doorbell ringing, followed by the ear-piercing sound of her miniature poodles yapping. Elaine did a quick check of her long blonde hair neatly tied back into a ponytail, and her expertly applied makeup in the grand gold-emblazed hall mirror. Then made her way to the double front doors, flinging them wide open.

"Michael darling, why don't you use your keys?"

"Mum, I prefer to let someone know I'm coming in, I didn't want to frighten you. Where's Julia, shouldn't she be opening the door?"

Julia is Elaine and Ben Pridemoore's housekeeper and has been since their children were in their late teens. Michael and Zac didn't care for her much at first, but later she became like a sister to them.

"Even the help gets a day off now and then, Michael." Elaine giggled.

"Oh Mum, you are *so* pretentious," they both laughed. The dogs had calmed down once they had a good sniff of Michael and retreated up the leopard print carpeted grand staircase, to Elaine and Ben's bedroom.

"Ben darling, Michael's here! Oh, there they are, how the heck did they end up there of all places? Ben, please remember to put my keys back where they belong. I just don't know what's gotten into you lately, mind like a sieve," Elaine scolded as she located her car keys and scooped them up with her well-manicured fingers.

"G'day Mike, how's it hanging?" came a voice from behind Elaine.

"Yeah, good thanks, Dad. How are you going?"

"Can't complain, no one listens away," Ben laughed.

Michael's dad, Ben, is quite the Aussie larrikin. People are shocked to learn after meeting him that he is a well-respected surgeon, one of the top in his field.

"Darling, your father and I are about to go to a surgeon something or other luncheon down Portsea way. I gather you are here to use the pool; it's a stinking hot day. Be a love and remember to lock up and put the alarm on when you leave, your father and I won't be back until later tonight. Can you feed Fluffy and Cujo as well and oh, there's some cash in an envelope on the hall console to give Paul when he finishes out there."

Michael walked further into the house and looked at the envelope on the hall console, marked in black ink in his mother's handwriting was the name 'Paul'. He stared at it for a moment as his mother and father began to leave.

"Hey, Mum, who's Paul anyway?"

"Didn't you see him when you came in? He's the gardener; he just started working with Bob, such a nice boy. I think you'll like him." Elaine winked and smiled at Michael as she and Ben left the house.

Michael headed straight for the kitchen, it was almost lunchtime, and he was hungry. He would often come and visit his parents.

He used to live in this house from around the age of five, just him, his brother Zac and his mum and dad. It was quite a big house for only the four of them, that's why his mother eventually employed a housekeeper to help with cleaning and so on around the house. She was five years older than Michael and Zac. Once they accepted Julia as part of the family, they all got on famously; she was the sister and the daughter they never had. She used to live-in until Michael and Zac moved out of the mansion. Once married, Julia also moved out to live with her husband just a few suburbs away.

Elaine has redecorated the house a few times since Michael moved out. Currently, the house is decorated in ornate French Provincial style. The kitchen especially, which features French doors opening out to the pool area.

Michael couldn't find anything quick to eat. The sight of the pool was becoming too much to bear. He was so desperate to jump in, have a splash around and catch some rays. Michael peeled off his t-shirt, folded it and placed it on a chair in the kitchen before opening the French doors.

The heat coming into the kitchen from the opened doors was stifling. Once outside he shut the doors to keep the heat out of the house. He slipped off his thongs, pulled down his shorts and stepped out of them. He dive-bombed into the pool with a big splash. The cool water offered him a great deal of relief from the summer heat.

As Michael surfaced from the water, he heard Fluffy and Cujo barking. "Oh Shit, Paul," he muttered aloud as he got out of the pool. Dripping wet he looked around for a towel and found one in the nearby pool house.

He made his way inside the main house, with the towel wrapped around his waist. Shooing the dogs away he opened the front door.

"Paul, I assume, from the Bob's Gardening logo on your shirt?"

"Yes hi, I'm Paul, you walked past me earlier and thought I was Bob, but I didn't get a chance to respond."

Paul was wearing a wide-brimmed hat and sunglasses, his arms and legs were pale, sweat dripped from his chin. It was hard to see what Paul looked like underneath the hat on his head. Michael felt as though Paul was eyeing him off, standing there in just a towel and still dripping with water. Michael always thought everybody lusted after him.

"Ummm, yes, here's the envelope with the money mum left for you." Michael handed it to Paul who folded it up and put it in his pocket. "Do you want to come inside for a cold drink? You look like you are melting."

"Yeah, I would love to; the temperature has just hit thirty-seven."

As Paul walked inside, he took off his sunglasses which gave Michael an excellent opportunity to check him out further. Paul looked right into Michael's eyes; Paul's eyes were a stunning blue-grey colour. Michael felt a shiver run down his spine. His heart began to gallop as an injection of adrenalin shot right through him.

Paul was slim and appeared to be in his mid-twenties, about five foot seven inches, but those eyes, Michael just couldn't stop staring at them. Paul seemed a bit uncomfortable as Michael led him into the kitchen. Paul took off his hat to reveal thick black hair which was sticking with sweat to his forehead.

"Nice place," remarked Paul.

"Thanks, this is my parents' house. I grew up here, but I don't live here. I have my own apartment a few blocks away, I don't have a pool, and I love to visit my parents anyway."

Michael filled a glass with ice cubes and poured lemonade into it. All was quiet except for the hiss of bubbles from the lemonade and the ice cubes clinking in the glass. Handing it to Paul, Michael accidentally on purpose brushed Paul's hand and felt a spark. Michael looked the oddly arousing gardener in the eyes. Paul turned away and looked at the pool.

"Wow, looks awesome," Paul said innocently, not realising Michael was lining him up as his next conquest.

"You are welcome to join me for a dip, Paul."

"I don't think your parents would approve of me, the gardener, frolicking with their son in the pool."

"No worries, they won't be home until late, and I'm sure they wouldn't mind. Mum thinks you're cute." Paul looked down nervously. "Come on then, let's get out there," Michael said excitedly.

"But I don't have anything to wear; I could go in my jocks I guess if that's okay with you?" Michael ripped off his towel in a dramatic fashion revealing his underwear and a big smile. Paul didn't appear to show any interest in Michael at all, much to Michael's bemusement. He didn't notice any longing stares at his well-toned gym fit body nor was he laughing at any of the lame jokes Michael told. Michael had surveyed almost every inch of Paul's pasty white skinny body; it looked like it had never seen the sun.

CHAPTER FOUR:
The Storm

After some time enjoying the cooling water of the swimming pool and floating around on the giant pink inflatable flamingo, they laid on the pool lounges to dry off.

"Boy, it's still pretty bloody hot once you get out of the water."

"Yep, sure is," Michael replied.

"Looks like you're a bit of a gym bunny, your body looks amazing. I bet you spend most of your life in the gym."

'*There you go,*' Michael thought, '*he did notice me.*'

"Well, I guess I do. I also go for a run most days, I love to run, it gives me time to think, and I feel free."

"Free of what, this lifestyle?" Paul responded sarcastically waving his hand towards the pool and perfect garden surrounds.

"Well no, I do get stressed just like everyone else you know. I'm a nurse, and I deal with a lot of awful situations every day." The annoyance in Michael's voice was crystal clear; he was tired of everyone thinking he had everything handed to him by his parents, even if it was the case.

A cool breeze broke the rising tension in the air providing much-needed relief from the heat and the conversation that was about to escalate.

"Guess that must be the cool change coming through," Michael said to steer the conversation back to being civil.

"Wow, right on time as predicted by the weather girls, let's hope it starts raining men," Paul joked. They both laughed laying there in silence for a while longer enjoying the cooling breeze. Dark clouds began to roll in as a loud crack of thunder made Paul jump and grab his chest.

"Well, that's our signal to go inside," yelled Michael just as the rain came pelting down.

Fluffy and Cujo came running downstairs into the kitchen where Michael and Paul were closing the French doors. "Oh, cute dogs, what are their names?"

"Well, this one is Fluffy, and the other is Cujo. Don't ask. Dad thought it would be hilarious to name such an innocent, harmless pup something ferocious. Mum didn't like it at all, but it's kinda funny. Dad thinks he's a comedian, well he is kinda funny, but don't ever let him know that or he won't shut up."

"You're lucky to have such nice parents. Your mum's so nice to me, though I've only met her twice. The way things are going with Bob's health I might just be taking over the business from him so you might be seeing me hanging around your parents' house more often."

"Well, that's another excuse for me to come over here more often."

The bucketing rain had reduced to a shower.

"Guess I'd better get dressed and get going. So nice to meet you, Michael, and thanks so much for your hospitality." Michael's heart began pounding; the adrenalin kicked in again. He was helpless from this foreign feeling. He felt powerless. There was no controlling the force pulsating through his body.

Michael escorted Paul through the house to the front door. Michael stood at the front door, not knowing what to do or say. He wanted to act on these odd feelings; he longed to hug and kiss Paul, he wanted to see Paul again, soon. Paul didn't appear to be interested in him in that way.

Michael took a deep breath and said, "Hope to see you again soon Paul."

Paul just smiled, nodded, and jogged over to his ute. Standing at the front door, Michael watched on as the light sprinkling summer rain fell gently on Paul.

Paul wasn't Michael's type at all, with his freckled parson's nose, thin villainous lips, and slight acne scarring on his cheeks. Something was alluring about him, not just his eyes; it ran deeper than that.

Michael questioned why he felt such strong sensations towards Paul. He had never felt that way about anybody before.

'Is this what love feels like?' he wondered. *'Is this sensation something deeper than looks? But what's more important than looks?'*

That was how he was brought up by his model mother; everything had to be beautiful to the eye. If something wasn't pleasing to the eye, it could always be fixed, or thrown out.

Paul drove through the light rain, windshield wipers intermittently wiping away the water and offering a clearer view of the road ahead. He wondered what his future could or would hold.

He had no plans for the year ahead; it was just two weeks into the new year, he didn't believe in new year's resolutions. He had to make plans to get himself out of the mess his life became. The mess he'd created for himself.

It's always easier to blame others, which he did at first. Once the haze had cleared from his mind, he knew he was the one to blame for his downward spiral. He could do this. He could gradually and entirely turn his life around.

As he drove over the West Gate Bridge on his way home, he looked at the suicide barriers erected on both sides of the bridge. He smiled a proud smile recalling how he managed to get his life somewhat back in order before he threw it away completely.

Working as a gardener wasn't a career he would have aspired to, but he did feel a calmness he never knew tending to plants. Observing plants as they grow, admiring their beauty and encouraging their development. The results could be seen and measured; this was just what Paul needed to turn his life around.

CHAPTER FIVE:
The Gym

The *clank, clank* sound of weights competed for noise space against the *thump, thump* beat of the dance music pumping through the entire gym. Dylan strutted out of the change room as if he were a catwalk model. Tiny red shorts showcasing his front and rear assets, tight white singlet, huge bicep muscles as big as the Andes.

Dylan was hot, and he knew it. Some would refer to him as a wanker. He strutted and paraded himself in the gym like he owned it and everyone in it. Life was good, better than good; he lived an amazing life. He was a doctor with his own practice; living in the Melbourne CBD in a stunning penthouse apartment.

The only thing eluding him was love. He loved himself no doubt, so perhaps there was no room for anyone else to be allowed in to love him. He'd had his share of guys, that wasn't an issue. A lot of them were looking to be the trophy husband, to grab a share of Dylan's wealth and success they wouldn't otherwise be able to achieve for themselves.

Then there was his friendship with Zac. They formed a close and lasting bond during their university years. Both came from wealthy families, Zac from an Australian father, and a Swiss mother, while Dylan and his parents were Norwegian.

Both loved to study and soon became top of their class spurred on by continually trying to outdo each other. Dylan set up a GP practice while Zac worked at a hospital.

Michael was the younger brother by about two minutes but wasn't as academic as Zac. Michael still wanted a career in health so opted for nursing instead. During one crazy booze-filled night out, Michael and Dylan hooked up. They continued to see each other for three weeks until Dylan had to play the "friends" card.

The way to differentiate the twins was the three moles on Zac's right cheek forming the shape of a triangle. After Zac's murder, Dylan found it hard to look at Michael again without bursting into tears of grief and despair over the loss of his best friend.

Michael had an even tougher time. His parents, Julia the housekeeper, and of course Dylan, couldn't look or speak to him without a quiver in their voice or a tear in their eye. No one ever seemed to know the pain of the twin who remains living. The bond they shared from the day they were born was still there, Michael always felt as though Zac was around.

Both boys always got on well; they knew each other's thoughts, could finish each other's sentences and they supported each other all the way. They adored each other, dropping everything at a moment's notice when required. Their loyalty to each other was a trait many admired.

"Hey, Dylan!" Michael called out, "Mirror, mirror on the wall who's the hottest of us all. Me, bitch, now move aside." They both laughed.

"How's your day been mate?" Michael giggled.

"Hectic today actually, the practice is booming, I might have to expand the way things are going. Have you been back to work yet after the incident a few days ago?"

"No, not yet, still got a few days left on the medical certificate you wrote out for me, so I thought I'd take all the days off work. I want to ask you something." Michael ushered Dylan away from the mirror to a quieter spot in the gym, then whispered, "I was thinking about what you said the other day when you picked me up after I was attacked. You said the guy that drugged me must have thought I was Zac. If this guy knows Zac and can remember him from almost two years ago, then maybe he could give me some information about his association with Zac. The police still have no leads on who murdered Zac and, instead of calling them and embarrassing myself over my ordeal, maybe we could try and find this guy."

"Sorry mate, did you say you want to find this guy who drugged and threatened you and who knows what else he did to you when you were unconscious? OMG, Michael, he might have taken nude photos of you and wants to blackmail you for them," Dylan said in a serious tone, desperately trying to hold back laughing out loud.

"OMFG! You could be right; I didn't think of that." Michael whispered.

"I wouldn't be too worried Michael, I'd say every male in this gym and most of the boys at the club have already seen you naked."

"Bitch! So, are you going to help me find this guy or not? We could totally be like detectives; I might have to wear a disguise and all."

"Okay, why not, sounds like fun, you come up with a plan, and I'll play along." Dylan sarcastically replied. He was used to Michael's grand schemes and dramas, they never lead to anything, and it was fun to play along.

"Michael, what's up with you today?"

"Nothing. Why?"

"Well, the guy that just walked past is the second one in the last five minutes that's given you the eye, I can't help but notice you turned away again. Usually, your eyes are wandering around so much you don't give me any eye contact when I'm speaking to you. So, tell me what's happening."

"How about we get to our workout, isn't that the reason we are both here, in a gym, surrounded by weight machines and barbells?" Michael replied rather dismissively. Dylan knew when he was being put back in his place and when to back off quizzing Michael but couldn't help but get in one last quip.

"Oh, I thought it was your never-ending quest for trade that brought you here?"

"Just spot me, cow." Michael retorted. "Come by my place tonight, say seven, all will be revealed."

"I can't wait, hope it's juicy," Dylan laughed.

* * *

Seven o'clock on the dot and the buzzer to Michael's apartment sounded. Dylan was a stickler for time, also neat and tidy to an OCD level. Dylan made his way up to the penthouse apartment in South Yarra where Michael lived, just a few blocks away from Michael's parents' house in Toorak. Michael's parents insisted on purchasing him his South Yarra apartment. It offered them some peace of mind knowing Michael was as safe as could be tucked up in the security this apartment complex provided.

The leafy, well-heeled, inner-city suburb of South Yarra is one of the safest and most affluent areas in the state of Victoria. It was his parent's anxieties about the safety of their remaining son which prompted the move from Michael's much-loved Californian bungalow in Kew to South Yarra. He didn't mind at all, he loved his parents dearly and living a short distance from them which meant he could spend more time with them. He realised how deeply traumatised they were over the death of Zac, as was he.

"Wine time bitch!" Dylan chimed holding up a bottle shaped brown paper bag as Michael opened the door to his much-loved visitor. Dylan kissed Michael on the cheek and swanned into his apartment placing the bottle of wine on the black granite bench top in the kitchen.

"I'd never get tired of this view," sighed Dylan as he made his way through the lounge room and onto the terrace outside.

The sun was beginning to set, and Dylan's eyes scanned the panoramic view of the city of Melbourne in the distance. "I think that's my place over there," Dylan said pointing his finger into the distance.

Michael pushed the small drinks trolley out onto the terrace greeting this warm January evening. They both sat and took a sip of the wine and stared into the distance; it was quiet except for the bubbles of the spa dissipating after the power had been turned off.

"Okay, spill girl," Dylan said in the campest voice he could muster.

"I think I'm in love," Michael blurted out without having to be prompted further.

"Say what? Where did this come from? The other day I picked you up after being kidnapped, and now you are in love? Oh no, don't you dare tell me it's the guy who kidnapped you, like a Stockholm Syndrome type of thing? Oh my god. That's why you were so quiet in the gym today. Oh Michael, no!"

"Dylan, shut up! No, it's not him, relax. Mum and dad have this new gardener; his name is Paul."

Dylan interrupted, "No, you can't be in love with the hired help, it just won't work, he's just not on the same level as you."

"Shut up Dylan! Mind if I get a word in? Well as I was going to say, I don't know if it's love or not. I haven't been in love before; lust yes, love no. It's the weirdest feeling; he's like totally not my type. Skinny, pale, and pasty. Nice thick longish black hair and totally amazing blue-grey eyes. Thing is, when I met him I felt something like a spark. It was odd; like the universe delivered him to me. My heart skipped a beat, as cliché as that sounds, and I felt a jolt of adrenalin pass right through me. I have been thinking about it ever since. Is this love I'm feeling?"

"Well it could be, I guess. But did I just catch you saying you have been thinking about *it* ever since, not him? Are you only referring to the situation or this Paul guy?"

"Dylan, you always listen so intently. But I think I'm in love with him; you know, love at first sight and all. But he didn't show much interest in me, so maybe I am wrong. Should I pursue him do you think?"

"Absolutely you should, I've never heard you talk about anybody like this before. I think you should take a chance. At least find out if he likes you back. Even, dare I say, though he is the hired help." Dylan sniggered.

DAVID GOLDON

CHAPTER SIX:
The Wild West

In the western suburbs, far away from the glitz and glamour of the Pridemoore residence, Paul lay on his bed, eyes closed, hands behind his head, daydreaming about Michael.

Oh, what it would be like to live the dream, to live like royalty in the lap of luxury. To have a handsome man such as Michael by his side, together they would go to all the glamorous first-night openings in town. They would wear the best clothes and travel to exotic places together. Michael would make love to him in the highest thread count sheets and lavish him with the most beautiful gifts.

Paul snapped back into reality when he heard a baby screaming in the flat above his. The pedestal fan hummed displacing the heat of this hot summer weather. His eyes wide open, he stared up at the dirty ceiling of his one-bedroom rented flat. He had himself to blame for being in this predicament; it was those same grandiose dreams which led him to live a nightmare.

It wasn't always like this; he had quite a good life before this, he was determined to pull himself out of this situation. He'd had a taste of the high life he had desired so much, he got in too deep, and it spiralled out of control. The whole high life thing had led him to a dark and dangerous place; he fought hard and managed to escape its clutches before it consumed him entirely.

He had the epiphany he required to come to terms that he wasn't a bad person, after all, he just needed to love himself for being himself. It was impossible to be what everyone else thought they wanted him to be and once the money ran out, he was on his own. He had become a creature of the night and ran with the other all-consuming creatures that he despised. It was people like Michael who got him into that mess and here he was again, back with Michael's people. Maybe it was a lesson he had to learn; perhaps it was fate testing him to see if he would fall again.

Paul smiled to himself in the thought he had given Michael the false impression he wasn't interested in him at all. How he handled himself deliberately not laughing at Michael's jokes and being ever so careful not to stare too long at his amazing sculptured body. But what was the attraction he felt Michael had for him? No-one like Michael would ever look at a scrawny, pale nobody gardener. Perhaps it was in his imagination?

Paul's phone buzzed, it was a text from his boss, Bob. 'Can you go to Pridemoore house next Tuesday at 10?' Paul excitedly responded back. 'Sure, no worries, boss. Will do.' Paul then called up his caseworker explaining he won't be able to make their meeting as he is working that day.

* * *

"Hey Julia, are you and hubby coming to my Australia Day party?"

"I hope so, Michael. Riley doesn't work on public holidays, and your mum and dad don't need me here. So, I would say yes, absolutely, but you know, being married and all, I'll have to check with Riley." Julia said as she held up her hand showing off the big rock on her finger as it sparkled in the morning sun shining through the kitchen window.

Julia is an attractive woman, with long blonde hair, big doll-like eyes, five foot nothing and a golden bronzed tan (from a bottle). She is a perfect replica of a doll. But she didn't always look like a doll until the day Elaine Pridemoore waved her golden glamour wand.

Julia applied for a job as a housekeeper at the Pridemoore residence in Toorak over ten years ago. A short mousey brown-haired girl from an Italian background turned up for the interview, left with the job and a free mini makeover. Julia had a lot in common with Elaine, they both loved hair and makeup, fashion and accessories. Julia's appearance at the time told another story.

Elaine longed for some company around the big empty house during the day. Her husband Ben was at work, and Michael and Zac were at school. She was a little lonely despite running her modelling school and wanted extra help with the day to day running of the household.

Once Julia was employed, Elaine used her as a pet project for something bigger she had been planning in her head for quite some time. Elaine's dream became a reality when she accepted her first five students into her home business, the *Pridemoore School of Modelling, Etiquette and Deportment.* Elaine was well qualified to run such a school; a former teen model before advancing to the catwalks of all the major European fashion houses. Hailing from Switzerland, Elaine still has a hint of Swiss accent hidden among a variety of other accents she'd picked up on her travels.

The joyful chime of the doorbell rang throughout the house as if in surround sound stereo. Fluffy and Cujo raced down the stairs on cue barking loudly. Julia and Michael looked at each other with an expression reading 'which one of us is going to get that.' Looking at the clock, Julia said, "That'll be the gardener, your mother said he'd be here at ten o'clock."

"It's alright; I'll get it!" Michael squealed as he rushed past Julia. "Scram you two," he snapped at the dogs as they moved away from the door. 'Please be Paul; please be Paul'

Michael's hands trembled as he reached for the doorknob and turned it. He opened the door ever so slowly. He drew one hand up to shade his eyes from the bright sunlight streaming through the doorway. A figure stood in front of him surrounded by light like an angel had descended upon his doorstep. It was Paul.

"P-P Paul," he stuttered. With squinted eyes, he looked longingly into Paul's eyes, observing the thick jet-black hair sitting messily on his head. His pale white skinny arms exposed from the awful 'Bob's Gardening' polo shirt.

Michael was a mighty sight for Paul to behold; dressed in a tight branded t-shirt, well-fitting chino shorts and bare feet. Paul stood frozen for a few seconds, as did Michael; as if someone had pressed pause.

"Hey, Michael." A big smile came across Paul's face as he reached his hand out to shake Michael's. Michael reached out and took Paul's hand in his, squeezing it just tight enough to give off a masculine impression.

"Good to see you again, Paul."

"What a pleasant surprise to see you again, it's going to be another hot day today. Guess you are here to use your mum and dad's pool, right?"

"No actually, but you never know, I might stick around long enough if you want to go for a dip later," Michael responded flirtatiously.

Julia walked up behind Michael.

"Hi, Paul. How are you?" Michael jumped in fright not realising Julia was behind him.

"Good thanks, Julia, and you?"

"Awesome thanks. Elaine just wants you to mow the bit down the side of the house and trim up the topiaries. Once you're done, come back, and I'll give you the envelope Elaine has left here for you."

"Yep, will do. Catch you later, Michael." Paul said as he walked off to his ute.

"What was that?" Julia asked Michael quite excitedly.

"Damn you, Julia, I can't ever keep anything from you, you can read me like a book."

Michael glanced into the distance observing Paul's skinny white legs as he fussed about in the back of his ute. Smiling, Michael shut the front door and headed back into the kitchen with Julia following like a puppy right behind him. Julia smiled broadly at

Michael showing off her perfect white teeth. There was silence as Michael shot a dumb cheesy grin back to Julia. "I don't know; I don't know. There's just something about him."

"Hmmmm, I'm listening."

"I feel something unexplainable, something I haven't felt before. I'm drawn to him. I get a bit nervous when he's around, I shake, and I stutter, but the weird thing is, this is only the second time I've met him. Perhaps the universe delivered him to me for a reason. We did go for a swim here in the pool a while ago on that scorcher of a day, the whole time I felt nervous."

"Like butterflies in your tummy?" Julia asked.

"I guess so."

"Oh Michael, you are in love!"

"I am? So, is that what I'm feeling, love eh? But I'm not physically attracted to him, he's nice looking but not my type."

"Oh Michael, love transcends all of that. Besides, once the looks go, what's left? Nothing! But with Paul, you feel excited even without him having to be your type. So, it must be love. Oh, Michael, I am so excited for you, I think I'm going pee my pants," Julia gushed. Julia always oozed romanticism, and now she had a pet project to get Michael and Paul together.

Michael's phone rang, it was the hospital. "Damn, bugger, shit. I've been called into work. Sorry, Julia gotta go. Can't believe this, Paul's here, and I have to go to work, damn it, I'm spewing!" Michael raged.

"Get out there now and organise to meet up with him sometime. If you don't, I'll do it for you!" Julia threatened.

"I don't have time for it right now; I have to get to work as soon as possible. There's been a big accident, and they need all the staff they can get. Gotta go."

He quickly kissed Julia on the cheek before hurriedly leaving the house. Michael was disappointed he didn't see Paul as he drove away.

"Hi Julia, all done. I'm sure Mrs Pridemoore will be impressed with the job," Paul said when Julia greeted him at the front door an hour later. While Julia was standing at the door, she couldn't help but notice Paul's eyes darting around behind her.

"Michael had to go to work, guess he didn't see you before he left?"

"Uh, no, but that's okay, I just wanted to thank him again for last week."

"Oh," Julia smiled as she handed Paul the envelope Elaine had left for him.

"Let Michael know I'm sorry I missed him."

DAVID GOLDON

CHAPTER SEVEN:
The Party

"Hey mate, great to see you!"

"You too, Dylan. Come on in."

"Esky's over there for your wine; you know where everything else is."

"Michael, mate, look at the label on this wine. You think I'm going to put it in an esky for someone to scoff down? No way, this little baby I'm putting in your fridge, up the back hidden away from thieving eyes. You can, of course, have some, it's too expensive just for any riff-raff. And don't think for one second that I am going to be wearing any of that Australia Day stuff I can see over there. How embarrassing."

Michael laughed at Dylan.

Dylan was quite the refined type, he liked everything just so and made a hobby of looking down at others. His grooming and deportment were first class, he was Michael's best friend, and they got along famously despite Dylan's thwarted thinking that he was better than everybody else.

Michael's annual Australia Day party was in full swing; it was a perfect sunny afternoon for it. Guests were happily chatting outside on the terrace enjoying the slight summer breeze and a few drinks. Michael was running back and forth pushing the buzzer of his intercom system letting whoever buzzed it into his building.

"Julia, darling!" Michael yelled out in his campest voice across the room over the loud music.

"Oh Michael, you're drunk!"

"It's a party babe, let's dance."

"Hi, Michael. How are you? Plastered by the look of it, better save yourself for the fireworks in a few hours mate." A voice came from behind Julia; it was her new husband, Riley.

"Yay, fireworks!" Michael yelled while Julia and Riley laughed. Michael pressed the buzzer to let another guest into the building and went back to Julia and Riley.

Julia's eyes widened, and a smile came over her face. Michael looked over to see what had caught her eye. Walking sheepishly into the apartment, eyes surveying the room, was a smartly dressed nice looking guy.

"Oh fuckety, fuck, fuck, shit, poo, bum!" Michael said surprised after his eyes focused on the new arrival, realising it was Paul.

"Fresh meat," yelled out a suitably drunk Dylan as he made a beeline for Paul.

"You're not from around here, are you dear? I mean, those clothes and the shoes; canvas casual's, eeeek!" exclaimed Dylan in his wannabe drag queen voice.

"Paul!" Michael came rushing up to him, uninhibited he threw his arms around the shoulders of a shocked but bemused Paul.

"Oh, hey Michael, having a good time?"

"Paul, this is a surprise, a wonderful surprise." Michael cooed as he brushed Paul's hair from his forehead.

"Did you forget you invited me, you put a cute note along with an invitation in the envelope Julia gave me the other day." Michael started laughing and looked over at Julia while drunkenly hanging off Paul's neck.

Dylan interrupted, "Oh, so this is the ummm...errr... gardener, I'll leave you to it." With his nose in the air, he swanned off to the fridge to retrieve whatever was left of his expensive bottle of wine.

"So, Michael, nice place," Paul said allowing Michael to remain draped over him.

"I'll show you around, excuse us Jules, I'm gonna show this cute boy around my place," Michael slurred.

Julia turned and looked at Riley, they both laughed as Michael led Paul away by the hand.

Michael's apartment was full to its capacity with all types of different people, and many he didn't even know. Most of the guests congregated out on the terrace overlooking the Melbourne skyline on a beautiful warm evening.

"Well, bitch, all you do is fluff pillows and serve orange juice, I have to really work my butt off."

"That's what you get working for a budget airline dear; no first class equals no class." Julia heard two drag queens arguing.

"I love your hair by the way, is it horse?" They continued.

Julia had often mixed with drag queens she loved hearing all the humorous quips they would throw at each other. As she looked around for Michael, who should have finished his tour by now, she noticed people in all stages of undress in the spa; the music was pumping the atmosphere was joyous everyone was having a fabulous time. She hoped Michael wasn't spewing up, he doesn't usually drink much, but when he does, he's a happy drunk. Julia went inside and found Michael sitting on a sofa with Paul, they were holding hands and appeared to be having an in-depth conversation.

"Michael honey, the fireworks will be starting soon, you and Paul should come out onto the terrace now."

"Oh, yeah almost forgot, come on Paul, let's go outside." As the three of them walked towards the terrace, Michael laughed as he spotted Dylan wearing nothing but an Australian flag wrapped around his waist.

The fireworks were spectacular as usual. Standing behind Paul, Michael had his arms wrapped around Paul's waist and gently kissed the back of his head. Guests were cheering, laughing and screaming as the loud explosive noises of the fireworks echoed through the dusky night sky. Paul felt safe with Michael's masculine arms wrapped around him. There was no question now that Paul and Michael felt the same about each other.

After the fireworks finished, the dance music was cranked up. Dusk had turned to dark, and it was time for the creatures of the night to turn into the party animals they were.

Dylan was out on the terrace dancing, now wearing only his budgie smugglers emblazoned with the Australian flag on them accompanied by flag transfers on his perfectly formed pecs.

Julia found Michael in the kitchen pouring some champagne with Paul by his side. "Hey honey, me and Riley are leaving now, thanks for a great party."

"Yeah, thanks, mate, it was awesome," Riley chimed in.

"Nooooooo Julia you can't leave yet, you have to dance with me!" Julia looked at Riley, he nodded in agreement, and the two of them made their way out onto the terrace leaving Paul and Riley to chat.

While Julia was dancing with Michael on the terrace, she glanced inside the apartment to check on Riley; she noticed he appeared to be deep in conversation with Paul, so she could relax and enjoy her dance with Michael.

One of the drag queens was chatting to Dylan until her eyes shifted sidewards focusing instead on someone in the kitchen.

"What are you looking at, fancy someone in there do you?" Dylan yelled above the loud music to the drag queen.

"Do you know that short guy with the dark hair and questionable fashion choices, talking to the taller guy?" she yelled, pointing.

"Just met him tonight, he's Michael's parents' gardener, Paul I think his name is," Dylan yelled back.

"Oh, god it is too, Paul-pot-head they call him," she giggled. "I haven't seen him out in ages, and who's Michael?"

"It's his party; he lives here. I guess you came along as a plus one then?"

"Yeah, I came with the other drag over there. I'm an international flight attendant by day; I travel a lot. Wherever I lay my wig, that's my home. I've been away from Melbs for quite some time, but never fear this bitch is back now, fierce and sassy as ever. So be a love and point out to me who this Michael guy is."

"That's him out there on the terrace dancing with the short, pretty girl." Dylan pointed and yelled above the loud music.

Her eyes focused on Michael, her head jutted out for a closer inspection. She caught Michael's eye, and he waved, she gave a limp wave back at the same time Dylan waved. Feeling a little embarrassed she realised Michael was waving at Dylan, not her.

"I'm off love, going to do my Madonna show at the club!" She yelled. As she walked away, Dylan couldn't help but notice some awful undistinguishable tattoos on her arms.

CHAPTER EIGHT:
The Morning After

"Oh, my head is pounding, I'm never drinking again," Michael moaned as he turned to face Paul who lay in bed next to him.

"Poor Mikey's got a headache. But you did have a great time last night; it was awesome. Can you remember it?"

"Well, of course, I can, it was fabulous," Michael replied in a raspy voice.

The morning sun was peeking through the timber Venetian blinds in Michael's bedroom.

"Paul, are you naked, don't answer, I'll find out myself." Michael looked underneath the sheet to see they were both completely naked. Not allowing this opportunity to pass him by they both made love, despite Michael's pounding head.

Paul slowly slunk out of the one-thousand-thread-count sheets, tip-toed across the plush, velvety carpet into the en-suite. He slid the door shut so as not to disturb a still sleeping Michael.

Locating and flipping the light switch, he surveyed the surrounds and was taken aback by the luxury of the bathroom. Dark tiles covered the floor and walls, a huge double shower with perfectly clear clean glass, double vanity with brushed chrome tapware. Fluffy white towels under the vanity, a towel warmer on the wall not looking out of place in these luxurious surrounds. He looked into the full length mirror at his naked, pale, skinny body, his flat chest covered with a spray of dark chest hair. His black bed hair completed his look. He sighed.

'What am I doing here? I'm so out of place. Michael was drunk, that's why he insisted I stay last night. Look at me, yuck,' he thought as his inner voices ran through his head. *'Don't be so harsh on yourself; you have come a long way, you pulled yourself out of that mess you got yourself into. This is a new beginning for you. Stop doubting yourself. Smile, be charming and get on with it'.* He smiled a little smile still staring into the mirror.

Fiddling with the technology of the taps in the shower, he managed to have water cascading out of the huge shower and adjusted the water temperature. It was like standing underneath a waterfall; he stayed under the shower for longer than usual if he was at his own home, basking in the glory of the luxury he had always aspired to.

"They call him Paul-hot-head, she told me," Dylan laughed while speaking to Michael on the phone. "Better not get on the wrong side of him then."

"What else did she say?"

"Not much, she hasn't seen him in a while, she's an international flight attendant, in and out of the country quite a bit. Oh, and bitch, she's Madonna!" Dylan laughed.

"Is she the Madonna that performs at the club?"

"Yeah could be, she said she was going to do a show after she left your party. She came with some other drag; she asked who you were and when I pointed you out, she looked a little shocked and left in a hurry."

"Gotta go, Dylan," Michael apologised as he became distracted by Paul emerging from the en-suite.

"Is lover boy out of the shower? Tell me all the juicy details later, see ya."

"Well good afternoon, how was the shower?"

"Just amazing I could have stayed in there for hours," Paul confessed.

"Make yourself at home. I'll freshen up and shall we do lunch?"

'Gee Michael wants to do lunch with me, I thought he would just discard me like a used condom,' Paul thought.

He watched Michael as he got out of bed. He was even better looking than Paul remembered. His athletic muscle-bound frame and bronzed smooth skin clear from moles or freckles eroded Paul's self-confidence.

Paul got dressed, and while Michael was in the shower, he took the opportunity to snoop around. First stop was the walk-in wardrobe. It was like walking into a department store. Shirts hung on wooden hangers, his pants neatly hung up, and dozens of shoes which all appeared almost brand new. There was a large chaise lounge covered in dark chocolate velvet upholstery. A glass display case located in the centre of the wardrobe which wouldn't be out of place in a jewellery store. Watches in every colour and metal combination all locked behind shiny glass.

Paul reclined back on the chaise like Cleopatra, expecting any moment for a slave to feed him grapes. He heard the water of the shower stop; his fantasy ended abruptly as he quickly left the wardrobe and headed into the living room. It looked different to how it did last night with so many people milling around. The interior was masculine, dark shades with pops of various metallic shades. A silver photo frame reflecting the early afternoon sunlight caught Paul's attention.

He walked towards it and recognised the photo inside was a cheerful looking Michael. Smiling, he picked up the photo frame caressing Michael's cheek with his finger against the smooth feel of the glass. Looking at the photo, he realised he'd never noticed the three moles in the shape of a triangle on Michael's cheek. Then he was overcome with an awful urge to steal the photo frame which encased the image of his new boyfriend.

"Ready then? Let's go!" Michael's voice echoed through his apartment. A startled Paul dropped the photo frame onto the floorboards. There was no disguising the noise it made as it made contact. Paul bent over and snatched it up; luckily, it wasn't broken, he quickly returned it to its place.

Michael, not noticing Paul's obsession with the photo, looked around his apartment. "Julia did such a great job cleaning this place up; she's one amazing person. I didn't hear her come in or leave this morning" Michael gushed. Paul felt a bit disheartened, here he is, the hired help sleeping with the boss's son.

"Hey, do you mind if I change into some clean clothes of yours? Mine are a bit smelly and creased after you ravaged me last night." Paul laughed.

"Sure, no worries," Michael responded, "Help yourself," he pointed into his bedroom. Knowing there was no way he would fit into Michael's pants, he took a pair of crisp pressed dress shorts off the hanger. Taking a moment to feel the texture of the fabric and admiring the perfect stitching, he put them on; they were a perfect fit around the waist. Admiring how good they looked on him in the full-length mirror, then the next task of selecting a top to wear. Paul hadn't been inside a prestigious clothing store in quite some time, but today he felt as though he was and best of all it didn't cost him anything.

* * *

"Rabbit."

"Clown."

"Fluffy white duck."

"I can't see no fluffy white duck!"

Michael and Paul laid on their backs side by side, on the dewy grassy knoll. They stared up at the sky watching small clouds glide past. It was a warm afternoon. Michael took Paul's hand in his, gently squeezing it as they relaxed in a shaded area of the botanical gardens overlooking the ornamental lake. They felt a slight, tepid breeze flow around them as they stared into the sky above. Ducks quacking and the sound of children laughing came from the other side of the lake. They felt overcome with a sense of peace and calmness. Paul felt safe, secure, and loved. The sensation of the pressure of Michael's firm grip on his hand reaffirmed the unleashed, overwhelming joy he was feeling. He sighed as Michael whispered into the air, "Where have you been all my life?"

"Just waiting for the right time, I guess," Paul whispered back. "Are you feeling the same as me? Peace, serenity, and joy. I can feel it, for the first time in my life, Mikey, I feel it."

Michael released his grip on Paul's hand and sat upright. Looking at Paul lying beside him on the red tartan picnic rug, he moved his bulky frame over the top of Paul, lowering himself down anchoring his forearms to the ground so as not to crush Paul. Hearts were beating faster with a mixture of nerves and anxiety. They began kissing. The connection they were feeling was new, real, exciting, and overwhelming.

The impenetrable bubble which surrounded them burst. From the path, atop the knoll came a loud shout "Poofters!"

As Michael looked up, he could see the spineless homophobe running off into the distance. They both laughed. Michael, being the athletic type, could have caught up to this guy and beat him the crap out of him, but Michael wasn't that type of guy.

CHAPTER NINE:
The Assumption

Elaine sat slumped in her favourite deep purple velvet chair next to the huge window overlooking the manicured front garden. It was a beautiful sunny morning outside. Her elbow rested on the arm of her chair, her palm under her chin propping up her head. She felt despondent, staring out into the distance observing the birds fluttering about in the water fountain.

She wondered how best to approach the news she had just been given. Was it even her place to say anything? Perhaps she should keep quiet, but no, that wasn't her. The house was silent except for the faint noise of birds chirping outside and Julia doing some housework.

"What's wrong, Elaine?" Julia asked.

"Nothing dear, just thinking."

Julia knew something was wrong; it was out of character for Elaine to be like this. Julia knew Elaine would open up soon, so she stayed in the sitting room dusting.

"Darling," Elaine chimed, "you dusted there yesterday." Elaine motioned Julia to sit in the nearby chair. Elaine's gaze fell to the floor, she looked up at Julia and sighed. "Bob, you know, the gardener? Just got off the phone with him and he gave me some distressing news. First, he asked if I was happy with the work Paul was doing in his absence, to which I gave Paul a glowing reference, which he deserves." There was a long pause. Elaine looked up at the ceiling and then back at Julia. "Julia, Bob told me, rather reluctantly, that," Elaine took a deep breath, "Paul is a criminal!"

"What?" a surprised Julia gasped.

Elaine continued. "Yes a...a... criminal!"

Always loving some drama, Julia piped up, "Oh my god, did he murder someone?"

"Oh, no don't be silly dear, nothing that dramatic. Bob told me Paul was working for him as a part of a Community Order. It's like a punishment I guess instead of going to prison."

"What did he do? What did he do?" Julia asked.

"He's an embezzler."

Julia gave Elaine a blank look, Elaine explained, "He stole money from a company where he was working. Bob didn't know all the details and was a bit reluctant to let me know anything at all. But he did tell me Paul was an accountant, and so I gather he was syphoning funds off into his own account or something. Poor Michael, I wonder if he knows he has been seeing a criminal for the past few weeks."

Elaine stood up and began pacing back and forth in front of the window.

Julia remained seated with her head in her hands. "Elaine, what are we going to do? Will you tell Michael?"

"You know Michael, always so trusting, caring and a bit naïve. I don't know how he will take this news."

"Maybe he already knows and wants to keep it private? Paul seems like a sweetheart, and you know Michael; he is so kind and understanding, I'm sure he will be fine," Julia said.

* * *

"Yes, yes, yes. Almost there. Push harder. Harder!" Michael instructed Paul while spotting him on the bench press at the gym. "Well done Paul, we'll have you muscled up in no time, but you will be sore tomorrow and the next day."

"Better be worth it, Mikey. It was kind of distracting lying there trying to concentrate on lifting the barbell while looking up your shorts."

"Nothing you haven't seen before, perve! Now let's move on."

"Hey, Michael!" A voice shouted out from across the crowded gym. Dylan weaved his way past several workout machines when he reached Michael, and he noticed Paul sitting on the bench press. He nodded and gave a half-hearted smile to Paul. "How's it going boys? See you got a new gym buddy mate."

"Yeah, thought Paul could do with some beefing up."

"Have you been taking lessons from your mother's beauty school, can't help but notice the tan and haircut. Are you trying to turn him into a mini you?" Dylan laughed, not caring about Paul who was sitting right in front of him.

'Asshole,' Paul thought. He never liked Dylan from the moment he met him.

"You see the guy over there with the awesome tatt of a serpent going up his arm and the head of it ending on his back?" Dylan asked Michael.

"Yeah, he's hard to miss."

"Haven't you noticed him turning around looking at you flashing a sly smile?"

"No, not really. Paul and I saw him in the car park, he parked next to us, as we got out of the car he got out of his and gave us a nod. Isn't that right Paul?" Michael asked, trying to include Paul in the conversation.

Paul looked up and smiled at Michael while avoiding eye contact with Dylan.

"In fact, Paul mentioned he liked that tattoo so much he's going to get one, aren't you my sweet?" Michael laughed as Paul stuck out his tongue. "Anyway, we better get back into it. Paul, you get on the bike and do some cardio for a while, and Dylan and I will continue with the weights."

Paul stood up and bumped both Dylan and Michael as he stormed off between them and headed for the cardio area. He got on a bike as requested, adjusted the control panel, and began peddling. He peddled faster and faster the more he thought about how much he resented Dylan. He wasn't happy with Michael either, fobbing him off as soon as Dylan turned up.

Paul looked around the crowded gym; he could no longer see Michael or Dylan. Ten minutes later, thanks to the exercise bike, he had calmed down and was ready to get out of that joint. Gyms were never his thing; he only went at Michael's suggestion knowing how fond Michael was of all things health and fitness.

Paul was becoming quite impatient; he'd had more than enough of the loud music, the smell, and not to mention all the Muscle Mary's parading around like it was a dog show. He laughed to himself every time he saw someone flexing in front of the floor-to-ceiling mirrors. *'Wankers.'*

While making his way to the change room he kept a sharp eye out for Michael and Dylan. He couldn't see them anywhere.

'Maybe they are already getting changed," he thought. *'No, they, well Michael, would have come and got me first.'*

As Paul entered the change room, he had a flashback to the change room at high school and how he hated sports. The day he left high school was one of the happiest days of his life. At university, he was free of the restrictions of high school, he performed much better academically and succeeded in fulfilling his career objective; becoming a qualified accountant.

This changing room was very different from those days; this was an upmarket gym. He admired how clean everything was, as a fresh scent of bleach filled his nostrils. There weren't many guys getting changed. He headed for his locker and began to retrieve the key from the small compartment of his shorts. He heard running water and noticed some shower stalls and thought maybe, on the off-chance, Michael was in there. He put his locker key back into his shorts and walked into the shower area.

There were ten shower stalls along one side of the room. A bench seat took up the entire wall on the other side, above it, there were hooks with various pieces of misplaced articles of clothing hanging from them.   As Paul walked further into the room, he noticed a towel hanging over the edge of the last stall. He made his way closer to the stall and noticed it was Michael's unmistakable designer black towel with a gold coloured monogram. No one else was around so he thought he would surprise Michael by popping his head over the top of the stall and yell out something funny.

As Paul descended upon the shower stall, the sound of the water became louder, but there was another sound. Moaning. Horrified at the thought, with his heart pounding and his body shaking he knew he had to do it. Paul raised himself up on the balls of his feet and looked over the top of the shower stall. He saw two guys in the shower making out and saw a tattoo on the back of one of the men. A tattoo of a serpent.

He could no longer look and stepped back. Paul's heart was beating even faster than before; he felt a sharp pain in his stomach. He wanted to throw up. The guy from the car park, the guy who was staring at his new boyfriend in the gym, was now in the shower with him, his beloved Michael.

Thoughts were whirling through Paul's mind, *'How could Michael betray me, I knew I wasn't good enough for him, I just knew it.'*

Paul ran out of the shower room, over to his locker and sat on a bench seat trying to regain his composure. Holding back his tears, Paul worked as hard as he could to control himself at least until he was at home.

'Damn, Michael drove. How will I get home?' he wondered. *'How can I face Michael after this?'*

Paul was getting angrier and angrier at the thought of serpent guy in the shower with Michael.

'He will pay for this!'

Paul's heart was beating fast; he was short of breath, his chest was tight, he was about to have a panic attack and had to get out of there. He got up from the bench seat and marched out of the change room, through the gym, right past Michael and Dylan, and out of the front door for some fresh air.

Five minutes later Paul returned to the gym, feeling much calmer. He saw Michael and Dylan putting some dumbbells away.

"How'd you go Paul, enjoy it?"

"Yeah, it was okay," he replied while holding his anger inside.

'How can he be so relaxed like nothing happened? Bloody cheater, I'll just play along, and once we get home I'll confront him,' Paul thought.

The three of them went into the change room to retrieve their clothing. Michael and Paul didn't bother changing out of their workout gear, grabbed their bags, and left Dylan there.

In the car park of the gym, they saw serpent guy on the phone standing next to his car. His car had two flat tyres, and the windscreen was smashed.

Michael shook his head at the malicious damage. "He must have upset someone, probably an ex I'd say."

"Guess so," Paul responded, smirking to himself.

As they both got into the car Paul saw Michael's black and gold designer towel in the back seat; he hadn't taken it with him to the gym.

On the drive back to Michael's place, Michael observed Paul's index finger frantically drawing small shapes across the top of his knee. He reached over and grabbed Paul's wrist while steering the car with his free hand.

"Paul, stop!" Michael said. Paul looked at Michael in bewilderment.

"Stop what?"

"Are you anxious about something?"

"No, I'm fine,"

Michael let go of Paul's wrist; he knew this was a sign that something was upsetting Paul but decided to let it go this time.

CHAPTER TEN:
The Family

The aroma of roast lamb filled the Pridemoore residence as Michael and Paul made their way through the front door accompanied by the ear-splitting sound of the over-excited Cujo and Fluffy yapping.

"Mum, Dad, we're here!" Michael yelled out.

Michael's nose beckoned him to the kitchen, his favourite meal of roast lamb, vegetables and crispy roast potatoes awaited. Holding Paul's hand, almost dragging him into the kitchen behind him, Michael could feel Paul's slight resistance.

Paul felt uncomfortable, even though he had briefly met Michael's mum and dad many times previously at the front door when he came to do the gardening. But this was different for him; this situation felt surreal. He couldn't help but feel less than equal, perhaps not up to the task of impressing the Pridemoore clan.

'Will they judge me? Am I good enough for their son?' These were the uncertainties chipping away at Pauls' confidence.

"Darling, so lovely to see you, and you too, Paul! You scrub up alright, much nicer than the gardening uniform. Have you been working out, looks like you are getting a bit of beef on you? That stubble looks great on you too, quite distinguished." Paul blushed;

he wasn't used to anyone making such a fuss over him. Elaine's kind comments bolstered his confidence.

"Yes, I agree, you do look much better," Julia cooed.

"Julia do you think Riley will be much longer? I don't want dinner ruined."

"He's on his way, won't be long now."

Paul had a concerned look on his face at the mention of Riley, which Julia noticed.

"You remember Riley, my husband; you two seemed to be having an in-depth conversation at Michael's Australia Day party?"

"Yeah, I remember him, it'll be nice to see him again," Paul lied.

A crystal chandelier hung from the high ceiling generating a soft, radiant glow over the dining room. A single white candle in a silver holder adorned both ends of the table. The dinner table was immaculate, featuring a centrepiece of sweet-scented fresh flowers. Each place setting consisted of gold cutlery, white French linen placemats, gold lined napkins and three crystal glasses.

Elaine loved to entertain and always went all out to impress. She cherished her family, and this occasion was one of those times the whole family would be together. This also presented an opportunity for her and Ben to get to know Paul on a personal level.

Soothing classical music was playing in the background as Michael, Paul, Ben, Elaine, and Julia were seated at the large table in the sumptuous surrounds of the formal dining room.

"And when Michael told me he was a horse's hoof as well, I was beside myself. Not one, but both sons, Michael, and Zac! There went my plans to become a grandpa and have the family name carried on for future generations. Once I got over the shock, I figured, you know, it's fine if my boys are happy, that's what's most important. Isn't that right sweet pea?"

"Yes dear, that's right," Elaine rolled her eyes having heard this story many times.

Paul felt confused upon hearing Ben mention something about both sons. Michael and Julia looked at each other and cringed. Ben always became louder and louder as he told the same old stories over and over after consuming a few too many glasses of wine.

"When I was a boy growing up..."

"Dad, please," Michael begged.

"Son, your new beau here, Paul, hasn't heard this one." Ben fell silent, feeling deflated at not being able to tell his story. "So, Paul, where do you live?"

"Altona," Paul responded.

"Oh, Altona!"

Bad answer. Michael closed his eyes and sighed.

"I grew up just down the road from there, Werribee. My parents had a farm there, you know. All gone now, developers bought the land and built houses all over it. Not such a quiet country town now I hear. Have you been to the Werribee Mansion or the zoo? Hey Mike, tell Paul he's got to take you there."

"Sorry," Michael mouthed to Paul sitting beside him.

The doorbell rang, up leapt the dogs out from under the dining table running towards the front door barking. Julia stood up. "That'll be hubby!"

Paul sighed to himself; disappointed Riley had turned up.

As Riley approached the dining table Michael rose from his seat in order to shake his hand, Riley smiled and flapped his hand, ushering Michael to sit. "Sorry I'm late everyone, well this looks all quite fancy, is it a special occasion?"

"Nah mate, just a family sit down and feed, you know how the missus likes to fuss around," Ben answered.

Riley sat opposite Paul, he looked over at Paul and gave him a nod. Paul returned the nod as his eyes shifted upwards to Julia who was standing behind Riley.

Paul felt uncomfortable at the thought that Riley may have disclosed to his wife any details that he and Riley had shared in the past.

'Riley is a professional, and he won't have broken any codes of conduct and confessed anything to Julia. Surely?' Paul felt as though Julia knew something, something about him, the way she was looking at him tonight caused him to feel uneasy.

Elaine caught Julia's attention and motioned for her to leave the table. They excused themselves so they could meet in the privacy of the kitchen.

"If Ben would shut up for a minute we might be able to suss out Paul," Elaine whispered. "He'll quieten down soon, then head to bed like he always does."

"How do we get Paul to talk?" Julia asked Elaine.

"Perhaps bring up accounting things and see what he says."

"I don't know any accounting things; I'm just the housekeeper."

"No, you're not just the housekeeper."

Elaine and Julia continued bickering in hushed voices until Michael called out "Mum, Julia; we're leaving!"

Elaine rushed into the dining room. "Darling, dessert is about to be served; you can't leave yet."

"Mum, you should know by now I don't eat dessert anymore, I haven't for several years. Not getting a touch of old timers disease, are you?" He laughed.

"Darling, don't be curt to your mother. Mother knows these things; it's just some fruit with a dollop of ice cream. Hang on, would you rather one of those protein shake things?"

Michael looked at Paul, who motioned to the chairs where they had been sitting. "Alright Mum, we'll stay then, but you know this six pack takes a lot of work," Michael said lifting his t-shirt revealing his abs.

Elaine returned to the kitchen to work on her plan with Julia.

"Elaine, ask him about his job and how he knows Bob and things like that."

Elaine sighed. "I guess I could, but I feel a bit unsure about all this, look at my hands, they're shaking."

"Don't worry then, Elaine; I'll do it, just in casual conversation and see what I can get out of him."

Back at the dinner table Julia observed Paul toying with his mixed berries and ice cream. "You don't have to eat it, Paul."

"Oh sorry, I'm away with the fairies," Paul responded as he began to eat his dessert.

"So, Paul, how did you come to be working with Bob?" Julia enquired.

"He's a family friend, and I wanted a change of career. Bob offered, and I thought, yeah, why not."

Julia shot Elaine a quick glance.

Julia continued, "And what were you doing before the gardening stuff?"

"Numbers, I was a numbers man." Julia had a blank look on her face. "Accountant, I was an accountant."

Julia nodded, while Michael looked up at Paul in astonishment.

"What? An accountant? You've never told me that!" Michael retorted with annoyance in his voice.

"Well, you never asked!"

Ben interrupted, "Now, now boys, settle down."

"And you never told me you have a brother!" Paul replied.

"Well, you always clam up when I ask you about your past like you are hiding something from me!"

The bickering between Michael and Paul was becoming quite heated.

"Okay boys, enough!" Ben yelled. "Michael, Zac, go to your rooms!"

Everyone looked at each other and laughed. After a few seconds, there was complete silence at the table as they all froze realising the error Ben had made by calling out Zac's name. Elaine burst into tears, pushed her chair back, and left the room. Julia was glassy eyed as she looked over at Ben and Michael. She left the dining room in search of Elaine. Michael, on the verge of tears, looked over at his dad. Ben just sat there with a confused look on his face. "Where did your mother go all of a sudden?"

"Dad, you just yelled at me and *Zac* to go to our rooms."

"What? Don't be silly son. I didn't say that. Did I?"

CHAPTER ELEVEN:
The Cracks Begin To Show

There was total silence in the car on the drive to Michael's apartment. Stopping at every red light during the short trip exacerbated the awful silence and frosty atmosphere in the car. Neither Michael nor Paul uttered a word to each other after the shocking revelations uncovered during the dramatic dinner finale at the Pridemoore residence.

Michael observed Paul again frantically drawing shapes with his index finger on his knee, a sure sign Paul was stressed. This time Michael resisted the urge to reach over to the passenger seat and grab Paul's hand in an effort for him to stop this behaviour.

Michael was still seething about Paul not telling him about his former career, so he let Paul stew. Paul was angry and upset that Michael never revealed he had a brother and whatever it was that triggered the emotional reaction of the Pridemoore clan at the mention of his brother Zac.

Michael drove into the basement car park of his apartment building. As they waited for the elevator, Paul wished he had the keys to his ute in his pocket, so he could leave right away. Both men entered the elevator; silence ensued as they rose up without stopping to Michael's top floor apartment.

As they entered the apartment, sensor lights activated radiating a warm glow on the showroom like interior. The only thing on Paul's mind was to get to the bedroom where he had left his keys and hightail it out of there back to his miserable flat.

Michael walked right past Paul and into the bedroom. Paul thought he had gone in there to get his keys and throw them at him right before Michael would push him out of the door and he would be forever banished. Michael emerged from the bedroom wearing a singlet, running shorts and shoes. Paul knew this is what Michael does when he gets stressed; he goes running.

"Will you be here when I get back?" Michael asked with a faint sound of hope in his voice.

"Yeah, guess so," Paul responded.

Michael gave Paul a slight smile as he left the apartment, offering Paul a glimmer of hope that they will be able to work through the situation.

As soon as Michael shut the door, Paul reluctantly made his way to the small bar area. He surveyed the bottles on display. The thought of losing Michael haunted him; the only guy he'd ever had intense feelings for, the only guy who ever appeared to truly love him in return.

'When Michael returns home, it could all be over.'

Paul had to have something to dull his pain, he was weak and vulnerable, without hesitation, he poured himself a scotch, straight up. As he sculled it in record time, he could feel the burning sensation igniting his throat. Feeling no guilt, he poured himself another. A voice in his head started telling him not to have that next drink; he had come too far in his sobriety. He ignored it. His nerves steadied as he played out in his head the dinner party scenario which had unfolded less than an hour ago.

Paul thought to have another look at the photo he'd fawned over that first time he'd stayed the night. He swallowed another mouthful of scotch, walked over to the cabinet and picked up the silver photo frame.

Staring at the photo which he first thought was Michael, he now recognised that in fact, it wasn't. Three moles on his right cheek shaping a triangle, which he'd discounted on the first view, took on a new meaning. He studied the face, the way he had studied Michael's face as they had laid in bed together.

'This must be Zac. What's the big deal? Why did Michael and his family have such a huge reaction to the mere mention of his name?'

* * *

Dusk descended upon the inner-city suburb of South Yarra as Michael began his run. He knew where he would run tonight. He ran along a few back streets so as not to be run over by vehicles which may be backing out of their driveways. Como Park was the best place for him to run tonight. The park was more an oval than a park; he could run around it for hours if needed while he gathered his thoughts.

Around and around the oval he ran, like a dog chasing its tail. Thoughts of Paul's misguided decision to not reveal a significant part of his life to Michael, his partner of three months, swirled around in his mind.

A cloak of autumnal darkness was cast over the city, and it was time for Michael to retreat to his apartment to face off with Paul. All he could hear on his run back to his home was the *tap, tap, tap* of his feet hitting the pavement and the sound of his breath exhaling, *pssst*. The same sounds were repeating in perfect mechanical rhythm.

As Michael opened the door to his apartment, he heard breaking glass. His heart jumped in fright as he made his way to where the noise came from. He saw Paul bent over picking up the silver photo frame from the floor. As Paul rose, he saw all six feet of Michael standing there like he was ready to pounce.

"It's just me! It's just me!" Paul yelled out. "Sorry, I was just looking at this photo, and I dropped it on the floor, I might have scratched the floorboards a bit sorry."

Paul was in a bit of shock because it felt like the photo frame was ripped from his hands and thrown with force onto the floorboards in front of him.

"That's Zac," Michael said.

"Yeah, I realised just tonight, all the time I thought it was you, but on closer inspection, I can see slight differences between the two of you, apart from the obvious moles on the cheek."

"Sorry, I didn't tell you about him. It's painful for me to talk about. In the past when I've opened up about Zac, previous boyfriends have taken pity on me and I end up being smothered by them. I didn't want that this time around, I just wanted you to love me for who I am, not let my grief define me. Unless you're a twin yourself, you wouldn't understand the deep bond we shared. Sometimes, I swear I can still feel him around me," Michael choked.

Paul placed the photo frame back on the shelf, stepping over the broken glass and made his way to Michael. He embraced his partner as he sobbed, his cheek becoming wet with the sweat of the t-shirt covering his chest. He could hear Michael's heart beating fast and gradually returning to a normal rhythm.

"I love you," Michael whispered.

"Love you too, Mikey."

In the morning, they lay in bed staring up at the ceiling. Silence. Paul knew his partner was expecting answers from the questions he didn't have time to ask him last night. Paul wondered if he should break the silence and reveal the hidden titbit about himself or wait until Michael asks.

"About last night," Paul said breaking the silence.

Michael didn't move or respond, still staring up at the ceiling allowing Paul to continue uninterrupted.

"I was going to tell you about my past, I was just waiting for the right time," Paul paused. "Yes, I was an accountant before this gardening gig and I, well I...," Paul took a deep breath. "I got in too deep, and I couldn't get myself out of financial difficulties, so I did something dumb, something I regret. I stole money from the company I was working for."

Paul breathed a deep sigh of relief; it felt good to get this secret out of the way, at least. No way would

Michael be ready to hear the other secret he was guarding.

"Okay," Michael responded.

"And I got caught and charged, and because of my age and the circumstances, I was ordered to do community service with Bob instead of going to prison. I can never work in finance again and so looks like I'll be gardening for the rest of my life." Paul sighed.

"Okay," Michael responded.

"Okay?" Paul said bewildered. "You're not going to kick me out of your life?"

"No, well you learned your lesson, right? I'm sure you must have been desperate to do something like that. From what I know of you, you're a decent, nice guy and everyone deserves a second chance. Do you remember what I said to you last night?"

"Um, yes, that you love me."

"Yes, I do, I really do, there's something about you Paul; I'm drawn to you like no other. I ask just one thing." Michael paused, "Get into the shower now, 'cause boy you stink! You smell like a brewery!"

They both laughed as Paul got out of bed and followed instructions.

CHAPTER TWELVE:
The 'Arresting' Officer

"Not now Michael, I'm kinda busy."

"You can't be too busy for what I'm about to tell you."

"Michael, I'm with the police at the moment, so no, sorry, I can't talk to you now!" Dylan replied.

"Oh my God, Dylan, are you alright? What's happening?"

"My medical practice was broken into last night, there's a lot of mess, but nothing's missing. Druggies I bet, even though I have signs displayed around the clinic there are no drugs of addiction kept on the premises. Bloody druggies can't read! Anyway, I'll call you later."

Dylan hung up on Michael.

"Yep just looks like a run of the mill classic case of druggies looking for, well, drugs, Dr Svensson."

"Thank you, Sergeant, I thought as much, not the first time either. I'll organise to get the surveillance footage to you soon. Not that it'll help." Dylan replied sarcastically.

"Thanks, Dr Svensson. Will you be bringing the footage to the station yourself or if you would prefer, I can come and collect it from you later today?"

And there it was, that look, that tingling nervous adrenalin pumping look. Dylan stood amongst the rubble of strewn pieces of office furniture, upturned chairs, and scattered brochures advertising drug counselling services. Frozen in time for a moment, Dylan came back to reality.

"Yes, please, if you can come back here later that'd be great," Dylan responded trying not to sound too eager.

"Okay, Dr Svensson, I'll give you a call and organise a time."

"Dylan, my name's Dylan."

The sergeant smiled, not just smiled but *smiled*. That smile, the smile that always accompanied that look. Dylan knew this cop was interested in more than the surveillance footage and Dylan was interested in more than just handing it over.

"Easton." The cop said to Dylan with a gorgeous beaming smile which illuminated the cop's olive complexion and emerald green eyes.

"Sorry, what? You've eaten?" Dylan replied with a quizzical look on his face.

The cop, grabbing an eyeful of Dylan's biceps protruding from his polo shirt, responded with a slight girlish smile, "East-on, like eastern but spelt differently. Yeah, don't ask. My parents are a bit quirky. I've thought about changing it but, it's me now. You know, it'd be like changing into another person, and a lot of people like it. Do you?"

"Yeah, actually I do, it has a certain Je ne sais pas about it." Dylan flirted.

"Oh, you speak French, Dylan?"

"Nah, that's about it." They both laughed.

Easton broke eye contact and turned his head surveying the mess surrounding them. Dylan took this opportunity to have a quick look over his new-found friend. Easton was about six foot, slim and lean, biceps protruding from his short-sleeved police uniform, short buzz cut hair, broad shoulders, this guy must work out.

"Okay, well, Dylan, do you have a card or something?"

"Um, well not that I can find right now," Dylan said while motioning his arm over the mess surrounding them.

"No worries mate, I'll give you mine," Easton said in his deep husky voice, sending a slight quiver through Dylan.

Dylan observed Easton's hand moving past the handcuffs and gun fastened to his belt into the front pocket of his trousers.

'*Arrest me, officer. NOW!*' Dylan thought as he broke into a slight sweat on the verge of having a dizzy spell.

Easton retrieved his business card from his pocket. As he held it out for Dylan to take, Dylan couldn't help but notice Easton's hand trembling. Dylan, trying to steady his nerves, reached out and took the card from Easton's hand. Their fingers touched, and they both felt something like static electricity pass through them during the limited physical contact. A chill pulsated through Dylan; he looked at the card. Easton Barlow, Sergeant.

Dylan slowly spoke the words "I'll be in contact soon, Easton."

"I look forward to it," Easton replied rather too keenly.

Easton smiled at Dylan, turned and tiptoed over the kaleidoscope of mess caused by the intruders, and walked out of Dylan's medical practice.

Dylan sighed as he watched Easton get into his police car parked directly outside the front door. The police car pulled out onto the road and was gone, just like that. Dylan stared at where the police car had been.

'What was that?' he questioned. He felt something, something emotional, deep; deeper than he had ever felt before.'

"Once I clean up this mess, I'll call Michael, that's what I'll do,"

* * *

A patient was wheeled from the ambulance bay into the hospital's emergency department. Michael swiftly approached the patient along with his colleagues.

"Sharp force trauma to the head, with a stiletto," yelled the ambulance officer.

Michael instantly recognised the patient's face. In shock, Michael took a few quick steps back from the bloodied face; his heart raced as his eyes focused on the undistinguishable tattoos on one of the patient's arms.

"Michael! Michael! What's wrong with you?" yelled the attending doctor.

A nurse gave Michael a dirty look as she stepped in to replace him. The patient was wheeled away disappearing down a corridor and out of sight. Michael remained leaning stiffly up against a wall in shock...

"Michael, what the hell?" A look of disdain came over the face of Francine Rockbottom, head of the E.D and Michael's big boss. Michael was seated across the desk from her as she leaned back into her comfortable looking chair, hands clasped in front of her.

Silence.

Michael squirmed in his small uncomfortable chair.

"I'm waiting." Francine's expression said all Michael needed to know; she was not happy at all. Michael took a deep breath as Francine's eyes focused on his. He hadn't seen her face so close before. She was pretty, long auburn hair, tortoiseshell glasses perched halfway along her nose, slim, make-up free face, she looked about forty years old. There was a photo on her desk of two small children; her office wall lined with various certificates of this and that.

Michael began, "Sorry I freaked out."

Francine just sat there as if frozen, staring into Michael's eyes like in a hypnotic trance. Michael broke eye contact averting his gaze to one of the certificates on the wall while trying to think of what to say next.

'Should I blurt out the whole long, sad, sorry story or make something up?'

Michael was still embarrassed by what happened that night he was drugged and taken to someone's dingy apartment. He kept pushing those memories to the back of his mind every time they surfaced. He was the victim; he was the one who suffered at the hands of that wicked person, the same person he recognised as he was whisked into the emergency department. How could he assist the person that drugged him and did goodness knows what to him while he was virtually comatose. He never thought he would recognise that person again, but he did and here he was in Michael's place of work, covered in blood.

Michael's professional and personal lives had collided in front of his eyes driving him into a state of shock. The sight of the tattoo, that unidentifiable tattoo which had etched its self into his mind more than the face of the perpetrator had.

"Oh, for goodness sake Michael!" Francine snapped jolting Michael back into reality. "You're a bloody good E.D. nurse, let's just put this episode to rest, shall we? I want you to take a couple of days off and get your shit together and sort out whatever it is that's bothering you. Just don't bring it into work again, or I'll really give your arse a kicking!" Francine said with a smile on her face.

"S-S-Sorry." Michael remorsefully whimpered.

CHAPTER THIRTEEN:
The Big Move

During the drive from South Yarra to pick up Paul, Michael felt as though he was going to have a panic attack and not because he was driving over the West Gate Bridge into the so-called unknown dregs of the western suburbs. He began practising his deep breathing exercises.

Thoughts were churning around in his mind, *'Will it be okay? Is it too soon? I do love him, and he loves me, it will be fine, just fine.'*

The GPS in Michael's SUV announced he had reached his destination. He found a car park on the street, using the assisted parking option his SUV made a perfect reverse park in-between two beat-up cars.

Checking the street number on the block of flats, Michael knew he was at the correct address and wasn't impressed with the aesthetics of the street or the block of flats which housed his loved one. The gloomy, depressing look of the dark brick of Paul's flat, overgrown weeds covering the nature strips and front yards of dilapidated houses made him feel uneasy.

An obese man wearing a dressing gown, looking quite dishevelled, stood at the front gate of his house staring at Michael's car. Michael noticed this guy staring at him which made him feel even more uncomfortable.

Opening the door of his vehicle and stepping out onto the road, for a moment he caught sight of his designer leather boots, the conflicting contrasts of worlds made him feel out of place. Loud laughter came from the direction of the obese man, as much as he wanted to get right back into his car and drive as fast as he could out of there, he didn't.

Michael took his time as he walked towards the block of flats then into the dark, dingy stairwell and up one flight of stairs; a wet moist smell invaded his nostrils. He knocked on the brown door with its paint flaking off, thinking there was no way his beautiful boyfriend could be living here. The door opened, and there Paul stood with a big stupid grin on his face.

"Well, hello handsome, come on in," Paul seductively whispered as he opened the door up to let Michael in.

Michael took a few steps inside. The smell was better than the stairwell but only just. The ceiling partly covered in mould; two worn armchairs sat behind a beat-up old coffee table. A few cardboard boxes piled up against a wall were all the belongings that Paul had.

"That's it then, just these boxes," Paul said.

Michael looked confused. "Just these then? What about the furniture?"

"That's not mine; they came with the flat."

With a sense of relief, Michael let out a large breath. "Phew, cause there's no way they're coming with you to my apartment."

"You mean our apartment, Mikey."

Michael smiled, "Yes, our apartment, Paul. Well, let's get these boxes to my car then."

Paul was looking forward to moving in with Michael, in fact, he was over the moon about it. He was surprised Michael had asked him so soon into their relationship but, as Paul spent a lot of his time staying at Michael's anyway, it made sense for him to move in.

The baby upstairs began its usual screaming as Paul slammed the door shut on his old life. He walked down the stairs carrying the last box of his belongings and out into the bright, warm sunshine, his ears tuned into birds chirping, all positive signs to the beginning of his new life. Paul slid on his sunglasses and gave Michael a reassuring smile, moving in together was the right thing to do. Returning the smile to him, Michael still wasn't one hundred per cent confident about having Paul live with him full time; he'd never had a live-in partner before.

Even though Michael offered Paul to move in with him, there was still a nagging doubt gnawing away continuously in his mind. Had he done the right thing? He loved Paul dearly despite the slight unfounded fear that something dangerous lurked within his partner. He recalled what Dylan told him about Paul being known to his friends as a hot head. Michael knew he couldn't be right; his Paul was a soft and kind natured person much like Michael himself.

'Where are Paul's so-called friends and his family. He always deflects the answers when questioned about them. Perhaps that's a warning sign?'

Paul snuggled into his seat in Michael's SUV, caressing the soft grey calfskin leather upholstery. As they drove off the obese man was still laughing out loud, Paul turned and gave him the royal wave as

Michael planted his foot on the accelerator and they sped off to begin their new life together.

Nearing the front door to Michael's penthouse apartment, Michael said to Paul, "I'll need to organise to get your fingerprints."

"What for?" Paul replied with a hint of aggression in his voice.

As Michael placed his index finger on a small glass plate, the lock on the door clicked as it opened.

"That's why." Michael smiled while wondering about Paul's tone of voice.

Paul looked relieved. "Oh yeah, forgot about that." He laughed.

If Michael were a cartoon character, he would have just experienced a light bulb moment. Did he catch Paul off guard? Paul has seen Michael open the door using the fingerprint technology many times before; he thought his request would be obvious to Paul.

As the door opened a flood of sunlight shone through the large windows illuminating the apartment, shiny objects shot beams of light around the room; dust danced in the glow of the light.

"Shall I carry you across the threshold?" Michael asked, but before Paul could answer he was scooped up into Michael's muscled arms and carried into the apartment. Gently laying him down on the luxurious overstuffed sofa, he smiled, and they kissed. "Welcome to your new life."

"Thanks, Mikey, I love you so much!" Paul squealed.

Paul luxuriated in the glow of the sunlight while lounging on the sofa with his man beside him. He was now free of the chains that restrained him. He is ready to move on and enjoy the new chapter of his life. Free at last. Everything is coming together; he couldn't be happier. This was his second chance.

At the forefront of his mind a mantra was on repeat in his head, *'Don't stuff it up, and make wise choices.'*

DAVID GOLDON

CHAPTER FOURTEEN:
The Haunted

"Hey, it's a great day, let's go out and do coffee and cake somewhere! Oh yeah, I know, just a teaspoon of cake for you, Mikey."

Michael smiled. "Where do you want to go?"

"Somewhere different, let's just head towards the beach and find somewhere around there."

It was a popular day to be outdoors by the bay beaches, cars lined the streets, and people filled the footpaths. After some time, Michael found a car park a few blocks away from the main drag. As they got out of the car Michael surveyed his surrounds; he felt uncomfortable being surrounded by unkempt blocks of flats with rubbish piled up on some of the nature strips. He put on his cap and sunglasses as he and Paul began to walk to the shop and café area. They walked along the footpath fast paced to escape the dangerous environment as soon as possible.

A short distance ahead of them, they saw a short, scrawny, dishevelled looking guy walking towards them. They made no eye contact with him as he came closer. As Michael and Paul passed him, he bumped his shoulder hard against Michael.

"Watch it mate!" Michael yelled over his shoulder as he continued walking.

"You owe me $500, asshole!" The dishevelled man yelled back.

Michael stood still and turned around to face the guy. "Don't even know you mate!"

"Don't give me that bullshit, I want my money now or gimme what I paid for, asshole!"

Paul stood by his man, feeling uneasy about the altercation unfolding before him.

"Mate, I don't know you!" Michael stressed.

The guy pulled out a small knife from his pocket and lunged at Michael. Without a second thought, Michael grabbed the guy's wrist, flung him to the ground disarming him without much effort. Those self-defence classes were worthwhile after all.

The knife fell into the rubbish piled up on the nature strip.

Michael grabbed Paul's hand. "Quick just keep walking."

Paul was shaken and in disbelief and did as Michael instructed. They walked as fast as they could to the end of the street while looking over their shoulders now and then. The guy was still lying on the footpath as they headed around a corner into another street finally out of sight.

"Oh, shit Mikey, the car!"

"He wouldn't have seen us getting out of it, so it should be safe, well as safe as it could be around here. Let's still do what we came here for and by the time we get back to the car that guy will be gone."

After reaching the safety of the hustle and bustle of the café strip, they both felt relieved as the adrenalin that was pumping around inside them settled down.

They found an intimate little café, sat down, and stared in disbelief at each other.

"So, what the hell, Mikey?"

"I swear, I've never seen that guy before, and I certainly don't owe anyone any money."

"You're my hero, Mikey. Wow, busting those Kung-Fu moves, I didn't know you knew self-defence, you impressed me." Paul gushed.

Michael smiled. His thoughts were elsewhere; he was sure he didn't know his attacker. He wondered if it was a delusional former patient from the hospital.

A voice from behind brought his mind interrupted his thoughts. The cafe owner greeted them as she brought them two glasses and a bottle of water, "Hi boys, how are you this fine..."

Smash!

The bottle of water shattered as it dropped from her hand and hit the paving stones.

"Oh, my fucking god," said the shocked owner, "Where the hell have you been, Zachary? I thought I'd seen a ghost for a minute."

As she grabbed a menu from the table to fan herself, she pulled out a spare chair and sat down.

"Yeah, like, make yourself right at home," Paul said as he stared at the intruder in disbelief.

"This is my cafe, sweetheart!" responded the owner. Turning her attention back to Michael, she asked, "Who's this little smart-ass you have with you, Zachary?"

"Hang on a minute. This is my partner, Paul, and I'm not Zac. I'm his twin brother, Michael."

"Oh, that's such a believable story. Not!" the owner laughed.

"Well, it's true," explained a frustrated Michael, pointing to his cheek, "Look, no moles."

"Yes, I see. Amazing what they can do with lasers these days, but I don't think some of the locals will buy that either."

With a laugh, and a wave, she called the waitress who had started to pack up the empty outdoor settings, "Mandy, can you get these boys' coffees, please?"

"Sure," Mandy replied as she approached the table. "What will it be, guys?"

"Doctor Zachary will have his usual macchiato," the owner responded, "And what will you have... ah, sorry, what was your name again?"

"Paul. I'll have a cappuccino. Thanks."

"No," interrupted Michael, "I'll have a decaf latte with almond milk, please."

"What?" exclaimed the surprised owner as Mandy headed off to get the coffees.

"I told you," continued a now frustrated Michael, "I am not Zac! He's dead."

"Dead? Ha! Well, you sure know how to play a role well, Doc."

"Will you just listen to me? Zac was my twin brother, and he was murdered two years ago. I'm Michael; I'm a nurse. Zac was the doctor."

"Mikey," interrupted Paul, "Show her the pics of you two on your phone."

Michael reached for his phone. *'If this doesn't convince her, nothing will,'* he thought. He found the pics on his phone while Paul reinforced what Michael had said.

After seeing the photos, the owner conceded that she was not talking to Zachary after all.

As the coffees arrived, she apologised, "I'm so sorry guys. Very sorry for your loss, ah... Michael. Look, enjoy your coffees, they're on the house. I'll leave you to it and get on with packing up. It's almost closing time, but don't rush, okay? You both take care now. You hear me?"

With that, she was gone. They decided to finish their drinks and headed off without delay, just as Mandy returned to clean up the broken glass.

Michael and Paul, feeling on edge, walked the seedy streets longing to get back to their car as fast as possible without any confrontation from the residents. As they walked past a block of flats, a woman's voice called out.

"Back from the dead are ya?"

They both turned to where the voice was coming from and saw a woman wearing a dirty football jumper two sizes too small for her. A lit cigarette hung out of her lopsided mouth. Paul screwed his nose up at her as they continued to walk past.

"Hey, I'm talkin' to ya, Zac baby! Ya still ain't delivered whatcha said ya would and I ain't too happy 'bout it. Showin' ya face 'round 'ere again, did ya think we'd all overdosed? Ya got a bloody nerve!" She yelled out like a banshee. "Hey Pete, quick get out 'ere, bloody fuck-face Zac's showin' his dirty scumbag face again!"

Michael grabbed hold of Paul's hand, and they ran. Michael dragged Paul behind him in an effort to get away as fast as possible. As they got into the car, they fumbled with their seat belts and managed to strap themselves in. Michael wasted no time getting his car into gear as they sped out of the squalid and dangerous surroundings.

A couple of minutes later, Michael pulled into the kerb and stopped the car.

Paul yelled at Michael, "What the fuck are you doing, let's get the hell out of here. Those inbreds might be chasing after us!"

Michael turned, looked at Paul. "Let 'em."

"You have seriously lost the plot. Don't you remember a small matter of a guy pulling a knife on you earlier, not to mention that ugly bitch yelling stuff out at you?"

"Things happen for a reason, right? So, me ending up here in this scary area where I'd never usually venture, and those people mistaking me for my brother. I believe I'm here for a reason."

"I believe we should seriously get the fuck out of here, that's what I believe!"

"I was thinking. Those degenerates' all thought I was Zac, so they must know him, right? So, maybe they might know something about who killed him."

"It was probably one of them, now let's get outta here!"

CHAPTER FIFTEEN:
The Hunted

The sun began to set on the squalid surrounds, concealing rusted bodies of old cars left for dead out the front of derelict houses. The downtrodden occupants of those houses lived their meagre lives in the poverty-stricken streets. The only beacon in the now darkened street was Michael's polar white SUV, standing out like the proverbial dog's balls.

Paul heard Michael unlocking his car door.

"No way! Where are you going?" Paul cried out.

"You coming?"

"Shit, you're serious, aren't you?"

Michael got out of the SUV shutting the door behind him. Too scared to be left alone Paul got out and darted around over to Michael.

"Well muscles, what's your plan?"

"I'm going to go back to that woman, convince her I'm not Zac and see if she knows anything about what happened to him?"

Paul was hesitant to go back to the run-down block of flats to confront that hideous woman. He felt safe with Michael though, more so after witnessing him taking down the derro who tried to knife him earlier.

Dusk soon turned to night. Paul began to shiver in the brisk evening air; he snuggled up to Michael.

The men embraced, the warmth and the strength he felt coming from his boyfriend's body offered him the courage he needed to move forward with this ill-planned scheme. The men were aware of the danger which may unfold but made their way back to the street where the crazy lady had yelled out at them.

Michael was nervous; he wasn't sure what he was going to say to the woman or if she'd even listen. She could attack him. He knew he had to be brave. Dylan's taunts about Michael's supposed cowardice were echoing in his head, *'This is what Dylan would do. He'd go and confront this situation.'*

Full of new-found confidence Michael felt comfortable he could do this. This was an opportunity for him to prove Dylan wrong and awake the confidence and inner strength he knew he had. He wouldn't only be doing this for himself; he'd be doing it for Zac. The murderer must be found; the police were useless, so this lead he would follow up himself.

Hand in hand the men approached the block of flats where the crazy woman lived. Standing motionless on the footpath they listened out for her. There was silence. Michael's bravado was short lived as he jumped and gasped in fright as a rat ran out in front of them and into the rubbish piled on the nature strip.

The block of flats housed six units, three stories high with an exposed stairwell in the middle. There was a path which led around to the back of the flats. The men stood still grasping each other's hands.

"So, are you going to make a move or are we going to stand out here and freeze to death?" asked Paul.

"I'm just trying to work out which flat is hers. I think it's that one." He said pointing at the ground floor flat with light escaping through the edges of the blind framing the window.

"Okay, go then," Paul said, giving Michael a gentle push.

Michael took a few steps towards the flats. Paul let go of his hand "You don't need me. I'll just hang back here. You can do it, Mikey." He smiled.

Swallowing hard and taking a few deep breaths, he slowly made his way along the path and into the small front yard. The fluorescent light in the stairwell blinked as he neared the front door of the ground floor flat. A few flower pots filled with dead plants lined the wall next to the door. With his pulse racing, he reached his arm out to knock on the door. He paused when he heard raised voices coming from within the flat. A woman's voice and an effeminate sounding male voice were arguing about something. Michael put his ear almost to the door to hear what was going on but couldn't make out the conversation.

Taking a few steps away from the door he looked to the footpath to check on Paul; he wasn't there. Concerned about his whereabouts, Michael abandoned his plan to confront the woman. He strode fast paced out of the uncomfortable surrounds of the flats and back out onto the street. Paul was nowhere to be seen. Michael took out his phone and called Paul only to get his voicemail. Thinking Paul may have returned to the car Michael decided he would head there to check for him.

While standing out in the street waiting for Michael, Paul jumped as he felt a hand on his shoulder. He turned to see his old mate Carro, a tall, lanky redhead; a ghost from the past.

"You look good, man, even in the dark. Haven't seen you in ages, where have you been?" Carro asked.

"Cleaned up my act, I don't do that shit anymore, it ruined my life," Paul whispered in response.

"Oh yeah? Then whatcha doing hanging around a drug dealer's place?"

"What? Who's a drug dealer?"

"A fat old bitch who lives in that flat," Carro said pointing to the flat where Michael was headed.

"No, not here for that. Long story. Can't explain now. We'll catch up soon though. Yeah?" Paul said.

"The fat bitch owes me. I'm going to go around to the back door; she never opens the front. Guess your mate's new at this."

"Hey, do me a favour? Just wait in the bush over there and if I don't come out in two minutes go in and get me."

Carro jogged along the pathway leading to the back of the flats before Paul could answer. The two of them had a long history, Paul was happy to see Carro again but preferred to leave him in the past where he belonged. Paul didn't want Carro to get hurt so he did as instructed and hid in a bush not far from the back door. Paul was relieved to see Carro make his exit in less than two minutes.

"Any luck?" Paul, who was concealed by a bush, whispered.

"Nah, bitch is holding out on me."

"Listen, I just saw Michael heading back towards the car, he's going to panic if I don't head back soon," Paul said as he emerged from the shrubbery.

"Can you do me one little favour? For old times' sake?" Carro pleaded.

Knowing full well what his former best friend meant he said, "Sorry, no money."

"You don't need any; you know what I mean? There's pills in a box of washing powder she keeps on the kitchen sink; you can't miss it."

"Carro, no. I don't do that anymore, and besides, I've got to get back to Michael."

"But Paulie, please. Just this one-time. I haven't seen you in ages. I miss you."

Feeling sorry for Carro, Paul agreed. He asked Carro to hide in the bush and wait for him to come out of the flat. He said he'd run past and drop the pills to him then continue on his way to find Michael. Carro was not to speak and to stay in hiding until Paul had made his getaway.

Michael paced back and forth next to his car worried sick about Paul. Hearing footsteps running towards him in the distance he turned and recognised Paul heading towards him. Out of breath, Paul opened the car door calling out for Michael to get in. Michael did as instructed and locked them both inside.

"What the hell, where were you?" Michael yelled.

Struggling for breath, Paul commanded Michael to drive. As they began to drive away, they heard a siren approaching. The siren became louder. It was an ambulance. They watched as it turned and went down the street they'd just left.

"I should go and see if they need a hand," Michael said as he stopped the car and unfastened his seatbelt.

Out of breath, Paul replied, "No, please, let's just get out of here!"

Michael turned to Paul and said, "Sure, I guess they don't need me getting in their way. Hey, what's that spot on your face, looks like blood?"

Paul lowered the vanity mirror and looked at his reflection. The light illuminated his face. "Bugger looks like a pimple," he replied.

Michael started the car and drove off into the night leaving behind the scummy neighbourhood. Paul licked his finger, reached up to his cheek and used the saliva to wipe the red spot away.

CHAPTER SIXTEEN:
The Boys' Night Out

Dylan breathed in the aroma and took a sip of the sample of wine the waiter had just poured for him. Dylan nodded and smiled at the waiter to signal he was happy with the choice of wine. The waiter filled his glass, Dylan signalled for the waiter to also fill the glass on the opposite side of the table. The restaurant was dark, lit only by tea light candles on each table creating a somewhat romantic atmosphere. Looking out the window, admiring the city lights from the dizzying heights of this top floor restaurant, a reflection of a moving figure in the window distracted him. He turned and saw Michael making his way to the table. Dylan stood and smiled.

"Hey mate. How are you love?" Michael said while air-kissing Dylan on both cheeks.

"Great love, how are you? It's been ages," Dylan beamed.

Michael sat at the table opposite Dylan and took a huge gulp of wine. "Nice one, mate."

"Cheers then," Dylan smiled as they clinked their glasses together.

"Why are you so happy, Dylan?" Michael was confused. This wasn't like Dylan; he looked like the cat that got the cream.

"I'm in love, and he loves me too!" Dylan gushed.

"The copper? The one you thought was a stripper? What's his name again, Western or something?"

"Easton actually, oh and how's what's-his-name?" Dylan replied waving his hand in the air. "Have you kicked him out yet?"

"No, it's going okay living together, we get on fine, for the most part, he's just a bit messy, towels and clothes on the floor type of thing."

They enjoyed each other's company chatting nonstop for the next few hours; it had been a while since they had been able to talk without their partners nearby. Michael told Dylan about being mistaken for Zac, the knife attack and taking some time off work after seeing the guy that drugged him in the hospital. Michael at least had a name of the perpetrator after asking one of his work colleagues; it was Marcus Ciccone. Dylan said he would speak to Easton about it and see if he could dig out some information.

They had organised to meet their partners, Paul, and Easton, at their favourite nightclub after dinner. Michael hadn't been back there since the night he was drugged. It was with some apprehension that he had agreed to go there again. Dylan thought it would be a good idea to help alleviate Michael's fear.

Michael stripped off his formal attire in favour of his tight-fitting clubbing outfit, locked his car and walked the short distance to the club. Dylan who had also changed his outfit was waiting outside the club for him. Michael waved and smiled at Dylan who waved back. They walked past the long queue of clubbers waiting outside in the cold night as the door bitch waved them into the club. It was an advantage of being well connected.

Their bodies began to thaw as they looked around the club for their respective partners. Music was blasting out loud. Lights were flashing brightly, it felt like home.

Dylan looked at Michael, "It'll be alright mate," Dylan said squeezing Michael's hand then letting go. Michael felt at ease; his best friend was always there for him, he could always depend on Dylan. "I think that one's yours!" Dylan yelled to Michael over the loud music.

Paul was standing a few metres away surrounded by a group of three guys and a girl talking and laughing together. Michael thought it was odd, as far as he knew Paul never mentioned he had any friends. Dylan nodded to Michael to go to Paul. Michael approached Paul from behind and put his arms around Paul's waist. Paul jumped in fright after feeling large, muscular arms gripping on to him.

"Mikey!" He smiled, stood up on his toes and kissed Michael on the lips. "These are all my friends; I haven't seen them in ages." Paul began to introduce them.

Michael couldn't make out their names because the music was too loud, so he just smiled and nodded at each of them. Paul looked super happy to see him and wouldn't stop chatting. Michael was excited to see Paul as well, but Paul's excitement was a bit over the top. Perhaps he was showing off to his friends that he had bagged this six-foot Adonis who was out of his league. Michael glanced over to where he'd left Dylan; he wasn't there.

Paul grabbed Michael's hand and led him onto the dance floor. Wide-eyed with excitement, Paul was dancing like a maniac waving his arms around above his head. Michael guessed he must have been drinking with his friends while he was waiting for him to arrive. They danced for quite a while, Michael was thirsty and starting to tire, he motioned to Paul he was going to get a drink from the bar.

Michael was making his way back from the bar with two bottles of water. He walked back towards the dance floor when Dylan stepped out of in front of him.

"Oh hey, there you are!" Dylan yelled. Michael glanced over Dylan's shoulder and saw an Italian looking guy. "This is Easton." They both smiled at each other. Taking him by surprise, Easton planted a kiss on Michael's cheek.

Paul was standing right beside Michael glaring at Easton after witnessing the innocent kiss. A wide-eyed Paul was bouncing up and down in time to the music; he took a bottle of water out of Michael's hand and began sculling it down. All three men stared at Paul, astonished at the rate he was guzzling the water right to the last drop.

Paul gave Dylan a dirty look and mouthed "prick" under his breath. Grabbing Michael's hand, Paul attempted to drag Michael back onto the dance floor with him, but Michael wasn't having any of it. Paul headed off to the dance floor, leaving Michael, Dylan, and Easton behind.

Dylan and Easton laughed. "Mate, he's off his tits!" Easton said to Michael.

"He sure is!" Dylan chimed.

Michael looked confused. "Yeah, he's had a few drinks, I guess."

"Michael, mate, he's on drugs!" Easton said.

"No way, Paul doesn't do drugs, he knows how dead set I am against them, he's just had too much to drink, that's all."

"Michael, you're letting your emotions cloud your judgement. Hell, I'm a doctor, he's a copper, sorry, police officer, and you're a god damn nurse! We see this shit all the time. Wake up!"

Dylan put his hand on Michael's shoulder. "Listen, you are a good guy. Too good, truth be told. You always see the good in everyone which is a great thing, you know. You defend people's actions, and I love you so much, and as your best friend I am telling you that fuckwit is on drugs!"

Michael began yelling at Dylan. "Oh, yeah, so now's the part where you tell me you were right about him the whole time, isn't it Dylan? You never liked him anyway, or you just didn't like me being happy and having a boyfriend, a live-in boyfriend. Something you've never had!"

Michael pushed Dylan's arm off his shoulder and stormed off. Dylan and Easton looked at each other in disbelief.

"That was way out of character for Michael, and it's the first time you've met him. He's a real sweetheart. A lovable guy, one of the best." Dylan said, almost in tears. Easton comforted Dylan by taking his hand and squeezing it.

Looking into Dylan's eyes, Easton said, "I don't know if I should say anything, but I know that guy, he has form. He's known as Paul pot-head, notorious for taking and dabbling in drug dealing. I've charged him at the station; I don't think he recognised me." Easton said, hands motioning at his barely-there club wear. "He was some high-flying corporate finance guy he got a bit greedy and stole money for drugs and shit like that."

A surprised looking Dylan said, "Oh shit, I gotta tell Michael!" As he tried to push past Easton, Easton grabbed hold of his arm, looked him in the eye and said, "No, Dylan, you are not!"

Dylan could tell by the look on Easton's face; this was serious. He decided not to pursue Michael.

Michael stood at the edge of the dance floor watching Paul and his friends dance like crazy people in time to the music. They looked like they were having a great time, all smiling at each other. Perhaps that explains Paul's behaviour, he was just happy, enjoying himself with his long-lost friends, friends he'd never mentioned to Michael before. Michael was sure Dylan and Easton were wrong about their assumptions that Paul had taken drugs. Paul wouldn't do that, knowing Michael's stance on the subject.

The music was pumping out loudly; laser lights bounced off the mirror ball in the centre of the dance floor shooting beams of light across the room. Michael was no longer in the mood for dancing the night away; his thoughts kept returning to Dylan's words about him seeing only the good in others and making excuses for their bad behaviour. Sometimes people are just bad. Not Paul though, he loved Michael and Michael loved him, it would be the ultimate betrayal if Paul willingly took drugs.

Michael thought to himself in his professional voice, '*Distance myself from Paul for a while and look at his behaviour, detach myself emotionally just for a moment. If Paul presented himself as a patient what would my diagnosis be?*'

Michael jumped as he felt an arm against his back, a hand gripped hold of his shoulder. "You right mate?" came Dylan's voice blasting his left ear.

Michael wanted to cry but controlled himself; this was not the place for tears. "Yeah, fine, just in a bit of shock that you and your new buddy are ganging up on Paul. Look at him, Dylan," Michael said pointing to where Paul was dancing, "he's a sweet innocent guy having the time of his life."

"Yes, yes he is," Dylan responded trying to sound as convincing as he could. He had planted a seed in Michael's head now, job done. He decided to back off, feeling how upset Michael was becoming. "Let's dance bitch!" Dylan yelled dragging Michael onto the dance floor.

On the short drive back to their apartment, Paul was talking non-stop nonsense. Michael couldn't respond to any of the conversation so just kept his concentration on the road ahead. Now out of the nightclub, Michael could notice the change of behaviour in Paul. This excited non-stop babbling was out of character.

Once inside the apartment, Michael noticed Paul's pupils were more dilated than usual, and he was fidgety. Michael decided to go to bed but Paul wasn't tired, he needed time to wind down. Michael shut the bedroom door and went to sleep. Paul put his headphones on, dance music blasted his ears as he danced on his own in the living room.

CHAPTER SEVENTEEN:
The Lie

"Poor Dylan," Michael said to Paul who was sprawled out on the sofa watching some mind-numbing program on TV.

"Yeah poor, poor, Dylan, he's got looks, a great body, lots of money and oh, by the way, he's a doctor. The poor thing," Paul huffed in response. Flicking over a few more stations, then turned the TV off. "Hey Mikey, it's a nice afternoon out, let's get in the spa."

Michael stood with his hands on his hips, glaring at Paul.

"What?" Paul said shrugging his shoulders. "Oh, right. Dylan. So, I'll bite, tell me about poor old Dylan, did he break a fingernail or worse, he has run lines on his fake tan?"

To distract Michael from answering, Paul began to undress, tossing his t-shirt on the lounge then in slow motion moves he lowered his shorts until they dropped to the floor. Maintaining eye contact with Michael, he slid his designer briefs down until they fell to the floor. Standing naked, to full attention, he flashed a sexy smile at Michael, turned and while walking to the terrace outside purred to his lover, "Bring the champagne, see you out there sexy."

That's all it took for Michael to lose his train of thought, without hesitation he headed for the fridge to take out a bottle of champagne. The cork was released from the bottle with a dignified pop as a wild bubbling noise came from the spa.

Michael wasted no time in making his way out to the spa, anticipating the sexy time he was about to have with Paul. He handed Paul the bottle of champagne and pulled his t-shirt over his head throwing it aside. Unfastening his belt, he dropped his shorts and underwear to the ground and clambered over and into the spa.

Paul swigged from the bottle, allowing champagne to dribble down his face. Michael snuggled up close to Paul caressing him all over, kissing his neck passionately. Paul held the bottle above the bubbling warm water as his lover sent him into a state of tingling ecstasy. "I'll give you a champagne kiss?" Paul asked.

"I don't know what that is, but I'm up for it," an excited Michael replied.

Paul took a swig of champagne, holding it in his mouth. His lips met Michael's as he allowed the yellow frothing bubbles to escape his mouth and enter Michael's. Michael soon realised how to play this game as the men passed the liquid from mouth to mouth until one of them swallowed.

Paul had Michael under his spell, Michael couldn't resist Paul's sexual overtures; there was something about his lover which ignited his insatiable sexual desire.

In the throes of passion, Paul whispered, "Now what was it about poor Dylan you wanted to tell me?"

Michael, nibbling Paul's ear and licking his neck couldn't believe Paul decided now was the time to bring this up, and so didn't respond.

"Oh, Mikey, yeah that feels so good," Paul whispered, "Tell me about Dylan, yeah Dylan."

Michael pulled back, looking Paul in the eye. "Are you getting off on Dylan?"

"Mikey, isn't that what you two wanted, to share me?"

"God no! What are you bloody talking about?" Michael demanded.

"Dylan wants me too. I thought you knew. You two share everything and are so close, that's what he told me," Paul said trying to sound like a seductress.

Michael shook his head. The passion had died in an instant, all he wanted now were answers.

"No way, you're lying. Dylan wouldn't say that!"

"He sure did. Think about it Mikey. Why have you had so many failed short-term relationships in the past? I'll tell you why; it's Dylan. Oh, he may come across as your best friend ever, but he's jealous of you. I think he wants you all to himself and let's face it, why can't a hot guy like him ever find a steady boyfriend? Simple. He wants you, nobody else is good enough for you, just him." Paul said with a smug look on his face.

"Liar!"

"No, not me. Don't bother asking him either; you know he'll only deny it."

Michael climbed out of the spa, picking up his clothing from the ground and went inside the apartment. Paul sniggered to himself; his plan may just come to fruition, and that asshole Dylan would be out of their lives for good.

121

Sitting on his bed, Michael wondered if what Paul had said was true. He had wondered why Dylan never had a long-term partner and why he had issues with everyone he'd ever dated. Now it appeared he was going to have issues with Paul. Perhaps Paul was the only one ballsy enough to tell him what Dylan had been doing behind his back. He didn't want to believe anything Paul said, but maybe, just maybe he had a point.

"Mate, I'm gonna come over there and rip his fucking head off!" Dylan yelled in a fit of rage over the phone to Michael. "Why are you even telling me this? Seriously, you don't believe a word of it, do you?" he fumed.

"No," Michael replied sheepishly.

"You're not doing a great good job of convincing me, mate! That fucker is trying to turn you against me. I've had enough of his shit, I'm coming over there right now, and I'm gonna throw that trash out of your place and back into the gutter where it came from."

Michael swallowed hard; his voice trembled as he replied to Dylan's outburst with a simple, "Sorry, I'll deal with it." He hung up.

"Shit!" Michael jumped as he felt a cold hand from behind him grip hold of his shoulder. He turned to see Paul standing behind him as he sat on the bed, "I didn't see you come in."

Paul smiled, unwrapping the towel from his waist.

"Don't worry about him, Mikey, you have me. I love you. Now let's finish what we started in the spa," he smirked.

"Nah, not in the mood now."

"I told you he'd deny it, didn't I, Mikey? Because it's true, he wants to split us up. You hurt me out there when you called me a liar. I love you. I'd never lie to you. You know that, right?"

Paul knelt on the bed behind Michael and began massaging his shoulders.

Michael stood up and turned around, looking at his naked boyfriend sitting on his haunches on their bed.

"I don't think I believe you. I was trying to tell you Dylan's medical practice had been vandalised, but I gather you already knew that."

DAVID GOLDON

CHAPTER EIGHTEEN:
The Confrontation

The smell of disinfectant filled Michael's nostrils; he felt happy to be back at work after the one week's leave he was forced to take by the head of the ED. The week off from work did help take his mind off being confronted by the patient he recognised as his attacker from the club months earlier. He now had a name for him, Marcus Ciccone.

The first thing Michael did when he arrived back at the hospital was look up Marcus Ciccone on the hospital's patient database. A shiver shot through Michael upon seeing that Marcus hadn't been discharged yet. Delving deeper into the patient record he saw Marcus' home address. He had the idea to enter the address into a search engine; this would be a sure way to find out if he was the perpetrator. Looking at the map, he saw the park he ran to the morning after the incident.

Michael needed closure from the traumatic incident. No matter how much he tried to bury it deep inside his mind, it kept resurfacing. Michael knew he needed to be brave, step up and confront this Marcus Ciccone. Dylan would be proud of him.

'*Ciccone?*' Michael encountered a sudden brain flash; dots were joining up in his head. '*Ciccone, that's Madonna's last name. There was a Madonna impersonator at the club that night, she was paying me particular attention during her performance. That old guy even noticed. That violent hero. Those undistinguishable tattoos – that was Madonna out of drag!'*

Michael began slapping his forehead, "Idiot," he repeated to himself. He noticed his work colleagues giving him dirty looks. He wrote the ward details on a piece of paper, folded it up and placed it in his pocket.

Time moved fast during the busy day in the E.D. He didn't have much time to think about how or if he would confront Marcus 'Madonna' Ciccone. His shift had finished, he knew what he had to do. Once Michael made his mind up there was no changing it.

He took the piece of paper out of his pocket, looking at the ward information. Still in his nurse's uniform, feeling confident he marched to the elevator. He was going to have this out with Marcus; he wanted answers.

Enjoying the feeling of his new-found confidence, he walked fast-paced into Marcus' private hospital room. Marcus, with a bandage on his forehead, was sitting up in bed eating dinner. Marcus stopped, his eyes widened when he saw Michael standing at the end of his bed. He dropped his spoon into the bowl.

Both men froze. Michael recognised Marcus; he hadn't even thought of what he was going to say before he arrived. Marcus remembered Michael straight away.

Hiding behind his professional nursing manner, Michael began, "I'm Michael Pridemoore, a nurse in ED; I was there when they brought you in. I believe someone hit you on the head with a stiletto?" Inside

Michael was giggling, hoping it didn't show through his brave facade.

Marcus didn't answer. He just sat there in his bed, starring Michael in the eyes.

Marcus stuttered, "Uh, y-yeah that's r-right." The room was silent. There was tension in the air.

Michael continued. "Do I look familiar to you?"

"No, never seen you before!"

Michael took a few steps closer. Standing beside the bed, he towered over a nervous looking Marcus.

Menacingly staring his attacker in the eyes, he said, "Have another look!"

Marcus' eyes shifted to the ceiling; he began gasping for breath, tears streamed from his eyes.

"I'm so sorry; I'm so sorry!" Marcus gasped, tears flooding his cheeks.

Michael felt a strange compulsion to comfort him but remained stoic.

"I saw you at the club when I was on stage," he blubbered, "I was dressed as Madonna. You look a lot like somebody else; I thought you were him until I got you home and realised you weren't him."

"Weren't who?" a stony-faced Michael asked.

"This guy, I paid quite a bit of money for him to get me some, um... some happy pills," he whispered. "I hadn't seen you, I mean him, at the club for quite some time, so I had to act. I slipped some Rohypnol into your drink when you were on the dance floor. I waited around until it took effect and then made my way over to you. That dirty old man tried to get his hands on you, so I pushed him out of the way, got you out of the club, into a taxi and back to my flat."

Marcus began to regain his composure and continued, "I took your clothes off and tied you up on my bed. I still wasn't sure what I was going to do with you. I hadn't thought it through because I wasn't expecting to see you ever again."

Michael began trembling. The realisation of what had unfolded that night had suddenly become real. He could have been murdered. The stoic, brave face he was putting on began to crack as fragments of the night flashed through his mind.

Waves of anxiety began to slam against him. Standing there in the hospital room he had to face the fears he had been suppressing for the past few months. Every time that night came into his mind, he would push it out, never talk about it, refuse to acknowledge he was ever put into that vulnerable position.

Staring at Marcus sitting up in the hospital bed, bandaged head, and cheeks wet with tears. Looking at this weak, pitiful person, Michael couldn't help but feel sympathy for him. Conflicted between his caring, compassionate nature and his need to deal with the trauma this guy had caused him, he stood there in a trance.

"Hellooo?" Marcus said, snapping Michael back into reality. "Are you okay?"

"Um, yeah," Michael replied, still a thousand miles away.

"This whole thing has traumatised you, hasn't it? I can sense by your aura you're a nice, caring person; a decent bloke. I'm so sorry if my actions have anything to do with how you're feeling right now. That night, I wasn't myself. I swear I don't usually go around drugging and abducting people," Marcus said sounding concerned for Michael.

"I'm sorry, so sorry," Marcus cried.

Michael felt the need to hug this guy and tell him he forgives him, and he understands it was just a case of mistaken identity. On the other hand, he had put Michael through a lot of mental pain. Dylan's constant scolding also played through his mind. He could hear Dylan's voice telling him to grow a pair, stop being a doormat, fight back.

Marcus' tone of voice switched from concerned to emotional. "I didn't touch you I swear! When I got a good look at your face, I realised you weren't Zac; you just looked like him. A lot like him. He had three moles in the shape of a triangle on his cheek; you didn't. I was so ashamed. I untied you and waited for you to wake up. I didn't know how to explain my actions to you, and you would probably call the police, so I thought I'd make some stupid revenge scenario up. I mean look at you, surely you've done someone wrong sometime?" he blurted out without taking a breath.

Michael's ears pricked up hearing the name of his brother; he thought he was hearing things. "Hey, back up a minute. Who did you say I looked like?"

"Zac, his name was Zac. Um... do you have a twin brother by any chance?"

Michael's heart sunk at the mention of his brother's name. No way was Zac involved with drugs, he was a doctor, a respected member of the community and he was never short of cash. Then he remembered the crazy people from the afternoon near the derelict apartment building. Their words made him start to question everything he knew about his brother.

Confused and shaken, Michael had to get out of there, he could no longer think straight. He turned and walked out of the hospital room.

The revelations were too much for him to bear. It just didn't make any sense. Marcus didn't know Zac had been murdered, Michael felt some relief with that knowledge.

Right now, he had to get back to the safety of his home. Then he'd call Dylan and tell him what he'd discovered tonight.

CHAPTER NINETEEN:
The Betrayal

Winter had set in, so there wasn't much gardening work for Paul. His boss, Bob, had advised him to be aware winter was a quiet time for the gardening business, so he ought to save up his money to get him through the quiet times. Paul wasn't too fussed about the cost of living; Michael took care of almost everything. Living with Michael was a huge financial advantage to Paul.

Paul invited the friends he had reconnected with at the club over to the apartment while Michael was at work. Paul opened the door and welcomed his friends into the luxurious penthouse. All four of them gasped in admiration at the beautifully appointed apartment.

"Wow, you landed on your feet, got yourself a sugar daddy or what, girl?" the flamboyant red-headed Carro asked.

"No Carro, Michael isn't much older than me, you saw him. Remember at the club; I introduced you guys to him on the dance floor?"

"Darling, I don't remember much of that night at all, you know what I'm talking about!" Carro replied wiggling his nose and taking a loud deep breath. "What about you other three bitches, you remember seeing Paul's daddy? On second thoughts don't answer; you're all still strung out from last night."

Paul swanned about waving his hands in the air showing off the apartment to his friends. He took them outside to the terrace to admire the city views, though most of the city was covered in a blanket of fog.

"My nipples are standing to attention out here darling, let's go back inside," Carro said as he motioned Paul and the others back inside the apartment. "Let's get this party started. Now how do I work this sound system?"

Carro pushed a few buttons, and dance music began to blast throughout the apartment.

While Carro began dancing provocatively, the others grabbed some of the beautiful crystal glasses from the cabinet and poured excessive amounts of Michael's expensive scotch into them. The drunker they all got, the louder the music became.

Carro took out a bag of white powder from his man bag and emptied the contents onto the glass coffee table. He divided the powder into lines, so there was enough for everyone. Paul rolled up a fifty dollar note and sniffed his lines up eagerly, soon followed by Carro and the other three. They all began dancing around the table and on the chairs and sofa, throwing cushions around and laughing hysterically.

Carro spotted the photo of Zac in the photo frame and picked it up. Holding it out to Paul he said, "Oh, so this is lover boy, yeah I do think I've seen him before."

"No, that's not him; it's his dead twin brother, Zac. You can tell by the three moles on his cheek!" Paul yelled at Carro above the music.

"Did you ever meet him?"

"No, he died about two years ago, before I met Michael."

A little flashback suddenly hit Paul, then he continued, "But you know, now that you mention it, maybe I have." Paul dismissed the thought, blaming it on the drugs. "Put it back Carro, it gives me the creeps and turn it around, I don't want him to see me like this, it feels like Michael is watching me and he would kill me if he knew what we were up to."

"When does he finish work, he ain't gonna walk in anytime soon is he?"

"No way man, he's working a double shift so won't be home until later tonight, so it's party central here right now!" Paul yelled as he began dancing again.

As Carro went to put the picture frame back on the shelf, it fell out of his hands and landed face up on the floor. "Oops, sorry love, lucky there's no glass in it."

"Yeah, I dropped it myself once, and the glass broke, never did get around to replacing it. Eeerrr feels like he's looking at me, shove it in the drawer instead, I don't want no dead man pooping my party."

"The stripper's here, the stripper's here!" yelled Carro as he saw a tall, muscular, good-looking man enter the apartment.

Carro approached the tall stranger. He couldn't resist showing off with his sexy dance moves synchronised to the fast, loud beat of the music blasting throughout the apartment. As he began gyrating against this giant's leg, he recognised the face.

"Oh, Paulee!" he yelled. "I think we got a problem!"

Michael stood in the lounge area, stunned. He just stood there. His eyes darted around to look at the unfamiliar faces. A pale-faced Emo guy, long black hair protruding from his black beanie; a handsome looking dark guy and a plump girl. All of them, sprawled out on the floor in fits of laughter. Soft furnishings scattered all over the floor, empty bottles of liquor sat on the coffee table with what appeared to be remnants of white powder.

Michael's world turned upside down. He couldn't believe what he was seeing. Strangers in his home, his perfectly placed ornaments scattered and when he'd noticed the photo of Zac was missing, he felt intense anger growing inside him. He felt like he was about to unleash a tirade of verbal abuse at everyone. He didn't say a word. He walked calmly into his bedroom.

A few minutes later Michael returned. He was wearing a singlet top and running shorts with reflective stripes. Paul knew immediately what that meant. When Michael becomes severely distressed, he runs. He could be hours out there running in the dark, away from the troubles of his life. He left the apartment without saying a word. Paul knew he was in trouble. Deep trouble.

Michael was naive, gullible, and too trusting, he would always be able to come up with an excuse to explain away someone else's bad behaviour. Paul often played shamelessly on Michael's naivety, but he had a feeling this incident could tip Michael over the edge.

As the door slammed shut, Carro broke the tension. "Oh, god girl, he is one mighty fine specimen you got there, you are surely batting way above your average. Bitch, please, what does he see in a scrawny white boy like you, when he could have a sassy hot redhead like me?"

Paul turned off the sound system. "Everyone get out!" he yelled.

"Oh, touchy bitch! Look at the time; it's after seven, us bitches gotta get ready for clubbing tonight. You coming, Paulee? Nah guess not, you got a lot of explaining to do."

'Carro is right,' Paul thought, as he tidied up the mess his long-lost friends had made. Long lost for a reason too. 'Why did I invite trouble back into my life just when things were looking up? The party lifestyle was good while it lasted, well actually not that good when you don't know how to stop.'

Slipping back into old habits came too easy for Paul, he realised, 'All the work I've done to regain my life. I had an opportunity to clean up my act. I didn't have to go to Jail, I got community service working at Bob's Gardening. Then I met Michael, the love of my life, someone who cared for me, protected me, and gave me my self-confidence back. I have a lot to thank Michael for, and this is how I repay him.'

Paul decided he would wait until the morning and call his drug and alcohol counsellor, Riley.

CHAPTER TWENTY:
The Scene Of The Crime

"Righty-o, you ready?"

"Think so," a nervous Michael replied as he unfastened his seatbelt.

Dylan and Michael stepped out of the car and made their way over to the ageing building. As they walked through the dank, cold entrance to the apartment block, painful memories came flooding back to Michael as he recalled fleeing down those same stairs escaping his captor. Making their way up the staircase, they could hear a Madonna song blasting out. Dylan stopped, turned, and smiled at Michael standing on the step below him. "I gather he's home then."

Michael's heartbeat increased with each step he took towards his captor's apartment. Standing outside the apartment door, Dylan turned to Michael standing behind him and quietly said, "Be brave mate, I'm not gonna leave here until we find out what's going on. I know you already had a go at him at the hospital, but I think I can squeeze a bit more out of him."

Michael responded with a limp smile and a nod. Dylan clenched his fist and began banging loudly and furiously on the door, so the occupant would be able to hear him above the loud music.

"Open the door. It's the city police!" he yelled.

"Oh, shit Dylan, no," an embarrassed Michael whispered as a smug smile came over Dylan's face.

After a few seconds, Dylan pounded on the door again. Michael felt uneasy and worried, observing Dylan's aggressive behaviour. The guy living on the other side of this door did Michael wrong, Dylan was fiercely protective of Michael; he just hoped this altercation wouldn't turn violent.

The volume of the music lowered, the door opened slowly. Dylan immediately placed his foot against the door to prevent it from being slammed in his face. The men burst out laughing at the sight of a fully made up head of Madonna attached to the body of a potbellied man.

"Marcus?" Michael asked as a huge grin came across his face.

A shocked-looking Marcus recognised Michael from their two previous encounters and attempted to push the door closed but was prevented by Dylan's size eleven boot acting as a doorstop. Dylan aggressively pushed the door wide open. It banged loudly as it hit the wall behind it. Brushing his way past a cowering Madonna impersonator, Dylan made his way into the apartment. He turned and looked at Michael standing outside, taking the cue, he reluctantly entered the apartment. Both men screwed their nose up as they smelt a putrid odour.

"You hiding dead bodies in here, mate?" Dylan snapped.

"No, my flatmate flooded the bathroom, the carpet was all wet. It's still drying out," Marcus nervously responded.

The three men stood in the passageway silent for a moment. Michael felt uneasy about this whole situation; he hoped Dylan wouldn't lose his cool. They were there for answers; something, anything that could lead them to Zac's murderer. If it hadn't been for Marcus drugging and kidnapping Michael in a case of mistaken identity, they wouldn't have this possible lead. A lead that could result in a murderer arrested and closure for those Zac had left behind.

Michael closed the door behind them. Marcus became fearful at the sight of these two tall, well-built men forcibly entering his home. Standing with his back up against the wall, he anticipated any moment now he was about to be punched out by one, or both men.

"I told you everything I know when you accosted me at the hospital," Marcus said looking at Michael.

Dylan interjected, "Yeah, he told me that, but I think you're holding back, that's why I'm here. You're going to tell us everything we want to know; we're not leaving until you do. I'll use any means I have to, to make you spill your guts." Dylan menaced Marcus. "You don't like being threatened, do you? But you can dish it out, like you did on my mate Michael here, right? You upset him, and you upset me."

Michael was bewildered by Dylan's intimidating behaviour; it was uncharacteristic, but rather exciting and humbling having someone stick up for you with such bravado.

"I can't speak to you looking like that," Dylan reached over and took hold of the wig, attempting to rip it off Marcus's head. Marcus yelled out in pain.

"Let me do it," he said as he removed the pins fastening it firmly against his hair hidden beneath." Marcus removed the wig, holding it in his hand loosely by his side as Dylan's muscled body kept him pinned against the wall.

"That's a bit better, I can't threaten Madonna, she's one of Michael's idols," Dylan sniggered.

Right then, at that moment, everything clicked in Michael's head, Dylan was playing a role, the role of the tough cop. With a sense of relief that the situation wouldn't escalate into violence, well at least not on Dylan's behalf, Michael took the opportunity to play along as well.

"Now we're not in public, you're going to tell me everything you know about my brother Zac, aren't you?" Michael said to Marcus in the most threatening tone he could muster.

Dylan grabbed hold of Marcus's t-shirt, bunching it up, contorting his face into an aggressive pose, he pushed Marcus against the wall. Marcus was in shock at the situation unfolding but also sexually aroused. Two hot muscle guys in his apartment, one forcibly restraining him against the wall, it was like a fantasy come to life.

"Okay, already I'll tell you, I'll tell you," Marcus squealed like a pig. "Just let go."

Dylan released his grip on the t-shirt and stood back allowing Marcus a bit of room.

"He was selling prescription drugs; that's all. No biggie, don't know what all this fuss is about." Marcus said in an annoyed tone. "He was a doctor right, and he could get us what we wanted. It was prescription, so it wasn't the cheap rubbish you get on the streets.

He had quite a market for it too. It wasn't just me; a few others I know were buying off him as well. We'd just pay him up front, and he'd usually stop by later and drop off the prescription, it was easy. He seems to have disappeared from the grid; some people aren't happy about that, he took the cash and didn't deliver."

"Then I saw you," Marcus said pointing at Michael. "I was sure it was Zac. How was I to know he had a twin? You'd better be careful; there's a line of mighty unhappy people out there."

"Yeah, well, Zac is dead. You'd better make sure all your buddies know that. This guy," Dylan said while pointing at Michael, "is not Zac, you leave him alone. You got it?" An angry Dylan pushed Marcus back up against the wall.

"Okay, you don't need to get all pushy." Sounding concerned Marcus asked, "How did Zac die?"

Michael responded, "He was stabbed to death, it would have been a frenzied attack according to the police. I guess our assumptions were right, now we know he was dealing, it probably was some junkie." A forlorn tone formed in Michael's voice, "I guess you have no idea who it would've been by any chance?"

Marcus looked into Dylan's menacing steely blue eyes, "No, sorry, I don't." Then, looking at Michael, "I didn't even know he was dead, that's why I drugged you and brought you back here. I honestly thought you were Zac, well in the light of the nightclub you looked like him. When I got you back here, I could see you weren't him. He had those moles on his face, and you didn't."

Satisfied with the answers and that Marcus didn't know any more than he'd already told Michael previously, the men prepared to leave the apartment.

Marcus blurted out "Are you sure you don't want to stay, I'd be up for a hot three-way?"

They ignored him and left the apartment slamming the door behind them.

There was silence as the men made their way down the two flights of stairs and into Dylan's car parked out front. Michael sensed something had upset his friend but had no idea what. Sitting in the car Dylan didn't turn on the ignition.

"Michael, what the fuck was that?"

"What?" a confused Michael responded.

"You just stood there with a goofy look on your face, like you felt sorry for that dickhead. That scumbag drugged and kidnapped you. I can't believe you didn't report it to the police," a frustrated Dylan replied.

"He mistook me for Zac, no harm done."

"Sometimes you just wanna make me scream! Mate, you've gotta learn to stand up and confront people, they're taking advantage of your kind nature. Mark my words, one day that's going to be your undoing." Dylan breathed a heavy sigh. "Listen, you're a great guy, I love you dearly, you're the only family I have, I'll go to any lengths to protect you, but you've gotta learn to fight back."

"Mmmmm...," responded Michael.

Dylan knew Michael would never change. He reached for his seatbelt, stretched it across his chest and fastened it, Michael did the same. They drove off feeling confident that at least they had confirmation of Zac's unsavoury secret life, but disappointed they didn't uncover a new lead into the identity of the murderer.

CHAPTER TWENTY-ONE:
The Watch

Ben was frantically searching through a chest of drawers in the living room when Michael arrived at his parent's house.

"Dad, what have you lost?"

"Hi, son. Didn't hear you come in. I'm trying to find my watch. You know, the one your mother bought me for my sixtieth birthday."

"That really expensive one? Well, you better find it fast. Mum will hit the ceiling if you've lost it."

"Maybe I left it upstairs, but I always take it off and leave it here in this top drawer, always," Ben said as he began walking up the stairs.

Elaine poked her head around the corner.

"Guess you heard that then Mum?"

"Yes, I did. It's not the first time your father has misplaced something. Michael, I'm a bit worried, he seems to be getting a bit forgetful. I think he might be getting that condition where you forget things, what's it called?"

"Alzheimer's, Mum."

"Yes, that. I've spoken to Sally, she's one of your father's work colleagues, and she said he appears to be perfectly fine at work. So, I don't know why he keeps misplacing things around the house."

The concerned tone of his mother's voice made Michael feel uneasy. Is his dad displaying the first signs of Alzheimer's or dementia?

Michael recalled the time when things got a bit heated at the dinner party his mother had for him and Paul and how his dad yelled at him and Paul to go to his bedroom, except he thought Paul was Zac.

Later, Paul mentioned to Michael that he thought Ben could be displaying the first signs of memory loss. Michael was surprised he hadn't picked that up himself.

"I'll keep an eye on him today, Mum. See if I notice any odd behaviour."

"Thanks love. What time's Paul coming over?"

"Not sure Mum, we had a bit of a fight last night," Michael replied, his voice breaking up into a sob.

Elaine motioned him over to the sofa by the bay windows looking out to the perfectly manicured front yard. As Michael approached the sofa, Elaine noticed he was limping.

"Darling, you are limping! Leg session at the gym?" Michael braved a lame smile at her. "Oh, darling, so things are going that well with Paul!" she giggled.

"Mum, No! Eeeww!"

Michael told her about what happened when he got home from work the night before. How he walked in on Paul and his friends dancing and drinking, purposely leaving out the small detail regarding fragments of white powder on the table. Michael said he refused to speak to Paul after he returned from his two-hour run. When he got home, everything was back in its rightful place as if the whole troubling incident never happened. Paul slept in the spare room; it was the first time in six months they hadn't sleep in the same bed.

Michael broke eye contact with his concerned mother and looked out at the garden. "Does Paul still come here and do the garden?"

"Yes, sweetie, he does. Surely you would have known that? He's like a member of the family now, despite all that, you know, criminal business." Elaine whispered. "He's such a nice sweet boy, offering to feed Fluffy and Cujo when no one's at home. I just leave the door unlocked when he's here, so he can pop in for a drink or something to eat if I'm downstairs at my beauty school or Julia and I are out at the shops. I figure even despite his, you know, criminal past, if he lives with you then I don't have to worry. Well, I just hope he doesn't have any parties here when no one's home," she giggled. "Don't worry too much dear, your father and I loved to party in our day."

"Thanks, Mum, yeah I guess you're right, he just likes to party," Michael lied, knowing his mum would flip if she knew about the drugs.

The doorbell rang, Fluffy and Cujo bounded down the stairs, yapping loudly. Michael limped to the door, hoping it wasn't Paul. It was. After realising it was Paul the dogs ran back up the stairs, they didn't care much for Paul. Michael felt like running up the stairs with them. He wasn't sure how he was going to react; he would have to hide his emotional state around his parents. After lunch, when they got back home, he planned to unleash his feelings.

Paul stood at the front door, his nose, and cheeks red with cold. His thin villainous lips were almost breaking into a full smile as Michael came into focus. He was wearing a long winter jacket, scarf wrapped around his neck, leather gloves and a beanie. Michael recognised most of the clothes as his. Paul had helped himself to Michael's wardrobe. Despite Michael's anger over their unresolved issues, he couldn't help but notice how cute Paul looked all rugged up on this cold winter day.

"Hi Mikey, is it still alright for me to join you guys for lunch? Your mum kept insisting I come; didn't want to let her down."

"Yep, guess so," replied Michael shifting his gaze down, unable to look his boyfriend in the face.

Paul took off his winter garments and hung them on the coat stand. "I walked here, needed some time to think." Michael stifled a smile.

"Hey Mrs P!" Paul called out upon seeing Elaine seated on the sofa.

"Paul, I've told you before, call me Elaine. Mrs P is so undignified! I'll leave you two to chat; I'll be in the kitchen helping Julia prepare lunch." Elaine swanned into the kitchen leaving the men alone.

Michael and Paul sat on the sofa recently vacated by his mother.

"So sorry about last night, the guys just came over, and things got a bit out of hand, we were drinking and dancing. I was going to clean up the mess. I didn't know you were going to be home so early." Michael listened intently to his boyfriend waiting for him to mention drugs, but he didn't. Michael knew what he saw on the coffee table. There was no way Paul would be able to explain away remnants of white powder. His parents' house wasn't the place to discuss such things. Michael carried on politely while remaining aloof towards Paul.

After a long lunch, Michael, Paul, Elaine, and Ben were sitting in the living room making small talk. The doorbell rang. Fluffy and Cujo began barking loudly as usual and ran downstairs to greet the visitor. Julia opened the door; it was her husband, Riley.

After Fluffy and Cujo made a fuss jumping up and down on him, they retreated upstairs as Julia escorted her husband through to the living room to join the Pridemoore family. Riley smiled and nodded acknowledging everyone in the room. Bending over to kiss Elaine on the cheek he whispered, "Sorry to be so late, had a crisis at work."

"No worries darl, I understand," Elaine whispered back.

DAVID GOLDON

CHAPTER TWENTY-TWO:
The Water

The gas-fired pebbled burner was giving off a lot of heat in the sitting room. The coffee table which separated the two large sofas had all types of treats along it, at the end sat a French press full of coffee. Julia and Elaine tended to the new arrival, handing him a plate with an assortment of petit fours and a cup of steaming hot freshly pressed coffee.

Riley sat opposite Paul. They gave each other a knowing look, as they did everyone in the room happened to pick up on the familiarity of the look they exchanged. Julia had noticed it previously.

'*Surely,*' Julia thought to herself, '*Riley couldn't possibly be having an affair with Paul?*' She dismissed it immediately from her mind.

Elaine looked at Julia as Julia happened to look at Elaine. Without words, they knew what the other was thinking.

Michael also thought something was a bit sus, '*Paul has only met Riley a few times, and I was always there. Or was I?*'

Michael's hand was shaking as he lifted the coffee cup to his lips. The room went quiet.

Thoughts whirled through Michael's mind about Paul. '*Not only is he an alcoholic and a drug addict, but he's also cheating on me with Riley! No, it can't be true.*'

Conversations continued with light-hearted banter. Everyone was chatting and having a lovely time except Michael. He looked over at his boyfriend who was carrying on as if nothing was wrong, smiling and laughing with everyone.

All eyes observed Michael as his large frame rose from his seat; he furnished a limp smile as he walked from the room. Everyone else carried on chatting. He walked through the kitchen, stopped, and looked out of the French doors at the swimming pool.

Opening the door, he took a few steps outside into the cold air and stepped into the deep end of the pool.

His boots weighted him until his feet reached the bottom. The water temperature was tepid, bubbles slightly tickling his face as they made their way to the surface. It was quiet. There were no problems here in the water. No one mistook him for Zac. He was free of Paul. Free of work. Free. Michael's arms rose to shoulder height, he felt light, like he was floating out into space.

His new-found freedom was abruptly interrupted as he felt a strong force drawing him away from his seclusion. A bright light appeared.

Michael opened his eyes and saw Riley's face looking down at him. He heard screaming. It was his mum and Julia. He coughed and coughed, water purging from his mouth. Riley sat him up. All his family were there; he thought he even saw Zac standing behind Paul.

Julia ran into the cabana, quickly returning with two large fluffy towels. Ben and Riley helped Michael to his feet. His mother smothered him with kisses, hysterically muttering something to him. He was in a daze; his solitude interrupted, realising he was back in the real world, a world with problems he didn't create.

Elaine left and went upstairs to Michael's old bedroom to gather some clothes he had left there. She gathered enough for both Michael and Riley to change.

By the pool, Elaine handed Michael and Riley the dry clothes and ushered them both into the poolside cabana to change. Everyone else went back inside to the warmth of the house.

It was chilly inside the cabana. Both men removed their wet clothing, standing naked in front of each other while drying off. Michael's sizeable muscular physique dwarfed Riley's small, sinewy frame. Without warning, Michael stood in front of Riley, grabbing him by the shoulders, forcibly kissing him hard.

Riley squirmed and murmured unable to speak, Michael's mouth pressing against his. Michael's grip was strong. Eventually, Riley managed to wriggle free from Michael's hold. Michael was amused; smirking after noticing the encounter had titillated Riley.

"What the hell, Michael!" Riley shouted as he backed away.

"Why have Paul, when you can have me? Or aren't I good enough for you?" Michael yelled.

"What are you bloody talking about, mate?" Riley snapped back.

"I know you've been seeing him, don't deny it, that look you gave each other when you arrived!"

Riley began to put some clothes on as did Michael.

"Well, he's obviously told you, so, yes, I have been seeing him recently," Riley responded cautiously.

"Knew it! I just knew it! That slimy little turd! How could he cheat on me? I'm going to kick him out of my place tonight," Michael responded angrily.

"Hang on a tick, Michael. You've got it so wrong." Riley nervously laughed. "And I think I've just breached a code of practice. You Nong! Michael, what do I do for a job?"

"You're a counsellor or something like that."

"Bingo Michael. I can't say anything more, but you can figure it out, right? I've known Paul longer than you have. I was surprised to see him at your Australia Day party, and when Julia told me he was the guy you were seeing, I was glad. Paul needs someone like you in his life. You are a great guy, so caring and thoughtful."

Michael slapped his forehead. *'Yes, it makes sense, that's how they must know each other, Riley is Paul's counsellor. But counsellor for what?'* he wondered.

"So, umm, what kind of counselling do you actually do?" Michael asked sheepishly.

"That's something I can tell you; it's drug and alcohol. That's no secret; I thought you already knew? The rest of your family do."

A jigsaw puzzle appeared in Michael's mind, all the pieces slowly fitting together. It makes sense, but Paul never told him he had drug and or alcohol issues, he only knew of the embezzling charges. Slowly the layers of secrecy surrounding his boyfriend were unravelling.

There was a lot more to Paul than the supposed cute innocent guy he had fallen in love with. Michael's mind began drifting into what, if anything, he should say to Paul. He loved Paul dearly, and Paul should feel comfortable in confiding to Michael, he would do anything to help Paul out. He wasn't sure if to wait for Paul to confide in him or perhaps he should confront him. It did appear that Paul was slipping back into his old ways. Michael could rescue him from the possible downward spiral he observed Paul could be taking. Michael felt a slap on his back. He came back to reality.

"Let's go inside; it's freezing in here. Don't worry mate, I understand, and I won't breathe a word about the kiss." Riley smiled, knowing the kiss didn't mean anything, understanding the strain Michael was under. "If you need someone to talk to, and I think you should, you scared us all; I know this guy called Victor. He's a guidance counsellor. Pretty cute too!" Riley smiled as he ushered Michael out of the cabana.

Michael and Riley entered the house and were besieged by everyone hugging, kissing and generally make a fuss of the two men.

Paul held Michael tightly, looking up into his eyes a single tear welled and dripped from Paul's eye. He knew he caused Michael to lose the plot. He loved Michael dearly and knew he had to get clean again before he fell into the hell of drugs and alcohol. Michael was the best thing that ever happened to him, he was a reason, a sole reason he needed to keep away from the likes of Carro and his mates.

'No,' he decided, 'I won't let the skeletons of the past drag me back into the depths of the world I've taken a long time to escape.' He finally felt like he had a purpose and for all the faults he had, Michael loved him, and he loved Michael.

"Julia, have you seen my ring; I left it here near the sink as usual when we were preparing lunch?" Elaine asked.

"Last time I saw it, that's where it was."

Both women searched around the kitchen floor and countertops for Elaine's ring as the men made their way back into the living room.

"Son, what the hell was that all about?" Ben asked aggressively. "Lucky Riley noticed something wasn't quite right with you and followed you out there."

After a lecture from his dad, Michael felt it was time to leave. He still had no idea why he wandered outside and stepped into the pool. He did enjoy the feeling but didn't think he would do it anytime again soon. His mind was a lot clearer after speaking to Riley. He decided he could do this; he would be supportive and help Paul anyway he could.

"There it is!" Elaine cried out. Her ring was sitting on the coffee table peeking out from behind a plate in front of Ben. Ben looked confused as Elaine reached in front of him rolling her eyes, as she took the ring and placed it back on her finger.

Paul discreetly pointed to Ben, whispering to Michael, "Alzheimer's," as they got up from their chairs.

They said their goodbyes and left to go home.

Elaine and Julia were in the kitchen stacking the dishwasher after the eventful Pridemoore family luncheon. Julia noticed Elaine was unusually quiet;

her hands were shaking with each dish Julia handed her. Julia wasn't sure how to broach what she knew was worrying Elaine. After the dishes were all loaded into the dishwasher, it began dutifully washing them.

Riley and Ben were still in the formal lounge room chatting away giving Julia an opportunity to speak to Elaine. Julia took Elaine's hand. Looking into her eyes, she said, "Do you want to talk about it now?" Elaine nodded. Julia escorted her to the casual dining table which overlooked the pool area outside. Elaine stared at the swimming pool; tears began to flood her face.

"What's going on with my boy? My beautiful kind, gentle boy," Elaine sobbed into a tissue Julia had handed to her. "I'm so worried, what on earth possessed him to try and kill himself?"

"I don't think it was as dramatic as that; I think he just wasn't in his right mind. Maybe it was something to do with Paul, did you notice how they weren't all lovey-dovey today? I'd say they had a tiff and Michael, well, can be a bit of a drama queen at times. A ploy for attention, I think."

"I hope that's all it is. Yeah, you're probably right. We'll have to keep an eye on him. Oh, wait!" Elaine gasped. "Riley, ask Riley if he can have a chat with Michael and find out what's going on."

"Oh yes, great idea, I'll ask him tonight when we are at home," Julia responded enthusiastically. "There's something else I want to speak to you about," Julia cautiously said to Elaine, "About your ring that was under Ben's plate."

Elaine tilted her head to the side in response, "Yes."

"I did see it on the sink, where you always leave it. As we were coming back inside after the Michael incident, I noticed Paul hanging around the sink." Julia said choosing her words carefully. "I noticed a short while afterwards your ring was not there anymore. I just assumed you put it back on. After it appeared underneath Ben's plate, I thought it was odd; I never saw Ben near the kitchen sink at all. I think Paul took it and put it under Ben's plate."

"Really?" a confused Elaine responded, "But why? That doesn't make any sense."

"No, it doesn't. But I know for sure Ben didn't do it."

CHAPTER TWENTY-THREE:
The Intervention

Michael had been dreading going to visit Dylan at his Collins Street penthouse in the city. The tone of Dylan's voice when he invited Michael felt as though he was being summoned, rather than a casual catch up between best friends.

His heartbeat quickened as he was buzzed in from the downstairs lobby. The elevator doors closed shut; the elevator began to climb to the top without stopping, there was no going back now. Michael checked himself out in the mirrors; the lighting was great, so he snapped a selfie, the elevator stopped, doors opened.

"Maaaaaate!" Dylan yelled enthusiastically. Michael wasn't expecting to see Dylan waiting for him outside the elevator; he hadn't fully composed himself yet. As soon as Michael stepped out of the elevator, Dylan greeted him with a smile and a strong hug. Dylan was either drunk or, as Michael suspected, he was about to walk into an intervention. He imagined as soon as he set foot in the apartment, his mum, dad, Riley and probably Julia would all be seated in a circle ready to pounce.

He calmed his breathing and went inside. Silent and empty. He sighed with relief. Dylan put his hand on Michael's shoulder which filled Michael with dread.

This wasn't typical Dylan behaviour. He was motioned to sit on the sofa while Dylan poured drinks. Dylan sat and made awkward small talk.

'*Any second now*,' Michael thought. He knew this guy too well; he knew Dylan felt uncomfortable about whatever was coming next.

"So, mate," Dylan began.

Michael shuddered.

"I hear you went for a dip. With all your clothes on. What's up with that?"

An awkward smile came over Michael's face as he felt his cheeks redden. Taking a sip of his drink, he didn't respond. He knew what he did was foolish but didn't need any help, he wasn't mental.

Dylan began tapping the ring on his finger against the glass he was holding waiting impatiently for an answer. Elaine had called him and filled him in on the events during the family luncheon, pleading with him to speak to Michael and find out how he was doing.

Michael's attention began to wander, shifting his attention to staring intently at Dylan. He focused on his hair. '*Blonde. Dyed or natural? He doesn't have a hair out of place. His skin is so tanned I wonder if it's real or fake, looks good though. That skin is flawless for his age. His eyes are so bright and clear. Those lips. Luscious, full, kissable.*'

"Michael!" Dylan snapped, bringing Michael's focus back to the moment.

"Sorry, I zoned out, what were you saying," he asked innocently.

"Oh God, I'm no counsellor I'm just gonna say it!" Dylan stood up, looking down at Michael and retorted irritably. "What the hell's going on with you! It's this bloody gardening boy, isn't it? Nothing but trouble that one, I knew it from the moment I met him. He's no good for you Michael, why won't you listen to me? He's broken and it's not up to you to fix him, he's emotionally damaging *you*! Take a step back you'll see I'm right. In fact, you know it, don't you?"

Michael averted his gaze away from Dylan, knowing what he said was right.

Silence fell in the apartment.

Staring into space, Michael swallowed hard. Taking a large breath in, he said. "I just feel sad." His lips narrowed as he blew a stream of air into the distance. "Every day, I just feel sad. Paul isn't making things easier, you were right about him taking drugs, and he's drinking a lot too. It turns out he's a recovering addict, and Riley is his counsellor."

Dylan's eyes widened. "Oh, shit mate, I didn't know it was as bad as that. You're trying to rescue him, aren't you? You don't need to answer, I know you better than you know yourself."

"I umm…. I don't love Paul at all. I mean, I thought I did but…" Swallowing hard tears welled in his eyes.

'Don't cry, don't cry, be a man, don't cry.'

His lips quivered, "I guess he came along at the right time and I threw myself at him. I asked him to move in with me, I hardly knew him. I've made such a mess of things. I've messed up his life too. He was probably doing well before I came along." Michael formed a fist with his hand, repeatedly hitting his forehead.

"Mate, I admire how kind and thoughtful you are towards others; guess I could take a leaf from you. It always ends up being at your detriment though.

You're still grieving, and you've teamed up with Paul who's trying to get his life back on track. Let's get this sorted together, hey?"

Michael nodded smiling limply at Dylan. Silence followed for what felt like a few minutes as each man tried to get a grasp on the whole situation, thinking of a way Michael can get out of it.

The silence was broken by what sounded like sniffles. Dylan noticed Michael's shoulders rising and lowering, his head in his hands and realised he was crying. Dylan was taken aback; he hadn't seen Michael in such a state before. Not being the overly emotional type himself, Dylan felt compelled to comfort Michael placing his hand on his shoulder. The sobbing subsided.

Michael rose to his feet, facing Dylan, remnants of tears shimmered on his cheeks.

The men embraced.

"We'll work this out, don't worry. You're not alone, you'll never get rid of me. I love you mate." Dylan whispered.

They broke their embrace.

Michael gave Dylan another one of his dumb looking limp smiles. He knew he could always rely on Dylan; he would always look out for him.

Michael had to face up to the facts; Paul was no angel. But he was trying to change; he was trying to turn a corner and become a better person, who was Michael to stand in his way? Michael was saddened his boyfriend hadn't confided in him. He knew about the embezzlement charges which Paul had confessed.

It wasn't a significant issue for Michael; Paul had shown remorse. Paul, however, hadn't divulged his drug-fuelled past.

"Another drink?"

"Only if it's your best scotch," Michael replied cheekily. "I took a tram here, so make it a double."

Dylan screwed up his nose, "Eeerrrrrr, public transport, I should've had you sanitised before I let you in."

In a sombre tone, Dylan added, "Your mum is planning a memorial for Zac next week. Can't believe it has been two years already and the cops still haven't found the bastard who murdered him."

"Yeah, I know. One day they'll find out who it was, I hope. Remember when I told you how lately these dodgy types have been mistaking me for Zac? Well, I was thinking... What if I were to go back to that part of town? But this time with you and Easton; seeing as Paul and I didn't make any progress. I thought Easton could hide somewhere, and when they come for me because I know they will, you guys can jump out and beat them up until they tell you something."

Dylan laughed out loud. "Maybe in an idealistic world, but I'll let Easton know you may have a few leads. Hey, what happened to Madonna?"

"She's overseas, as far as I know. She's a trolley dolly so could be anywhere."

"Cool, I'll pass that onto Easton as well, maybe he might get something out of him that we couldn't. So, I guess your mum will be going all out for Zac's memorial again this year?"

"Yeah you know mum, she'll have the big photo up on an easel, flowers, a slideshow of photos and this year she's even going to show some home videos! Yep, I'm getting ready to be embarrassed. At least it's only family this year and you, of course, you are a part of our family, like it or not, meathead!"

Michael giggled while playfully punching Dylan's bulging bicep.

CHAPTER TWENTY-FOUR:
The Memorial

Classical music gently danced in their ears, the sweet aroma of fresh flowers dominated their sense of smell as Michael, with Paul behind him, entered the Pridemoore mansion.

Fluffy and Cujo bounded down the grand staircase to welcome the visitors. They jumped for joy greeting Michael; then as before, after sniffing Paul, they ran back upstairs.

'Those two act so oddly with Paul,' thought Michael. Then he dismissed it completely.

The house felt serene, at peace. Michael's mum, with a flair for the dramatic, had the double doors closed to the sitting room where the memorial would be.

Walking slowly down the staircase to greet the men, Elaine was dressed in a tight-fitting black knee length skirt, black blouse, accompanied with matching black heels. Michael wouldn't bat an eyelid if she appeared wearing a black veil like an old Greek woman in mourning. She kissed Michael and then Paul on each cheek, ushering them into the living room. Ben, Julia, and Riley were already seated there.

Once Dylan arrived, Elaine would commence the proceedings. The doorbell rang, barking started, Fluffy and Cujo bounded down the staircase once again. Paul opened the door. Dylan gave him a forced smile, a limp handshake then turned his attention to the fluff balls pawing at his legs. Michael rose from his seat, greeting Dylan with a bear hug.

Elaine called all the mourners to attention. They gathered at the entrance to the sitting room. Elaine dramatically flung open the double doors ushering everybody inside.

Michael baulked at the sight of the over the top memorial display. He turned and looked at Dylan with a big smile on his face. Dylan returned his smile with a knowing look.

Just as anticipated, a large mounted photo of a smiling Zac was sitting on an easel in the middle of the room. Large floral arrangements bursting with fragrance sat either side of the photo. Virginal white church candles adorned the room. The sofas had been shunted away from their usual location in favour of the padded French style chairs, which formed an orderly row in front of the memorial display. Looking out of place, a large projection screen was on the wall behind the display.

Classical music streamed throughout the house, which wouldn't have been to Zac's taste, preferring heavy dance music. But today was also about his mother and what she wanted. The pebbled gas heater did its job warming up the room, creating an ambient glow in the slightly darkened room.

Ben, Riley, and Julia took their seats on the right side, while Dylan, Michael and Paul sat on the other side. No one was quite sure why there was a gap in the middle of the chairs; it wasn't as if a coffin would be making a procession through them.

Elaine stood centre stage, tissue in hand. Dylan and Michael exchanged a mischievous smirk like naughty schoolboys. They managed to withhold their fits of laughter which would have ensured be it any other occasion. The men would never make fun of Elaine in front of her, especially as they were here to honour a twin brother and a best friend.

Their mood soon changed as Elaine began to speak about her beloved son. She recalled childhood memories of Zac and Michael's formative years; funny anecdotes were reeled off one after the other. Some things a mother never forgets, much to Michaels cringing. Paul laughed softly in all the right places, squeezing his boyfriend's hand gently while they turned and smiled at each other.

At what was a sombre affair, Michael couldn't help but feel overjoyed. His boyfriend on one side gently, lovingly, tenderly holding his hand. Dylan, his best friend, sitting on the other side with his hand on Michael's knee. Michael felt loved, truly loved. People cared deeply for him.

He looked over at his dad, Julia, and Riley, they caught his look, smiling warmly at him while his mother continued speaking. The love he was feeling towards him strengthened the bond with everyone in the room. He wasn't sure what his emotional state of mind would be today, it was always painful recalling the loss of his beloved brother, especially on the anniversary of his tragic death.

'The killer is still out there, out there in this world somewhere. How can they live with what they have

done? Why did they do it? Will they ever pay for it?' The same questions are always looping around in Michael's mind, but today he needed to quash them all, today was about his brother.

The lights in the room were dimmed further as images of Zac appeared on the projection screen. A jovial mood filled the room as those in attendance pointed and yelled at the screen when photos of the twins appeared. They were taking guesses at which one Zac was, and which was Michael. Michael himself wasn't even sure. Only a closer examination would reveal the three moles in the shape of a triangle on Zac's right cheek proving who was who. As the photos of their childhood swiftly passed by, the awkward teen years appeared, Zac's moles were now more prominent, forcing an end to the guessing game.

Paul's hand, still holding Michael's, became clammy, Paul let go wiping the moisture off on his pants. Michael glanced over at Paul noticing his knee moving rapidly up and down, like he was bursting to go to the toilet, or he was anxious, which he doubted.

Once the slideshow had finished, videos began to appear, so did the raucous laughter and finger-pointing, the game was on again. Paul's knee stopped its movement. The video's moved onto Zac's graduation from medical school; he was clowning around with Dylan.

Noticing a tear trickling down Michael's cheek Dylan squeezed his best friend's knee. Turning to Paul, Michael saw him drawing shapes with his finger on his knee, something he always did when he was anxious about something.

Elaine burst into tears and began wailing. Michael turned to Dylan each exchanging an eye roll. Elaine was in fine form today, always the centre of attention. Everyone rose from their seats forming a loose circle around her, hugs, kisses and kind words were exchanged.

Michael felt an arm around him; he turned expecting Paul to be comforting him. Instead, it was Dylan, of course. "How are you doing?" He asked with concern.

"I'm alright," replied Michael.

It felt good that Dylan focussed his attention on Michael, Michael felt the loss of his brother deeply, yet his mother was always the one seeking attention. Elaine snapped back into her usual self, announcing there will be champagne and finger food served shortly in the living room.

The men gathered in the living room while the women were in the kitchen fussing around.

"Is everything in place?" Elaine whispered to Julia.

"Yes, mother goose, the traps have been set," Julia whispered back.

"Mother Goose? Oh, Julia, that's awful, why did you call me that?"

"Oh der, Elaine, it's your code name, haven't you ever seen one of those old spy movies?"

"Oh Julia, you're so funny. Or should that be Baby Goose?" she said winking and nudging Julia with her elbow.

"Have you noticed Paul's acting strangely today?" Julia whispered to Elaine.

"Yeah; he seems nervous. Maybe he knows we're onto him; his ruse will finally be up!"

"His goose will be cooked."

"Oh Julia, stop it. I haven't even had one glass of champagne yet, and you have me giggling like a school girl. I should be feeling upset; this is the second anniversary of my son's death."

"Elaine, Zac would be overjoyed to hear you laugh and have fun, you two always hit it off so well, quite the comedic double act."

Before everyone arrived for Zac's memorial Elaine and Julia had hatched a plan to discover if Julia's hunch about Paul was correct. Julia suspected Paul was behind the incidents leading up to everyone believing Ben was exhibiting signs of Alzheimer's. Pieces of jewellery would either go missing altogether or turn up in odd places usually frequented by Ben. Cunningly the women placed some cash and cheap jewellery in areas they knew Paul would frequent. The plan was set, now all they had to do was wait to find out if he would take the bait.

Everyone was happily chatting away in the sitting room exchanging stories about Zac. Paul was feeling left out of the conversations; he continued to slyly pour himself glass after glass of champagne hoping no one would notice. Catching Elaine and Julia's constant stares, he began to feel uneasy.

He rose from his seat feeling slightly woozy, discreetly making his way to the bathroom. On the way, he noticed the odd piece of jewellery and small amounts of cash looking out of place on side tables, hall stands and the like. He continued on his way thinking nothing further about it.

In the bathroom, he noticed he was looking a bit bleary-eyed. Splashing his face and regaining his composure he made his way back into the living room.

Resuming his seat, he noticed his glass had been removed from the coffee table, a sign that perhaps Michael had noticed his overindulgence. Paul also observed some unusual behaviour between Elaine and Julia. The women were whispering and appeared to be agreeing on something before Julia left the room.

Returning a short time later, standing out of Paul's line of sight, Julia subtly shook her head indicating to Elaine that the items were still there.

CHAPTER TWENTY-FIVE:

The Road To Engle Byen

The dark, miserable winter's day was turning into night as Michael pushed the button on the remote control closing all the curtains in his apartment. Paul sat on the sofa feeling slightly hung-over after all the champagne he indulged in at the memorial earlier in the day. The television was on without sound because his thoughts were elsewhere.

"Chinese?" asked Michael.

"Um, yeah, thanks." came Paul's short response.

"Are you okay, Paul? Thanks for coming along to Zac's memorial today, it meant a lot for you to be there for me. You would have loved Zac, he was a great guy and an awesome brother, but I was the better-looking one!"

Paul faked a smile. Michael picked up his car keys, making his way out the door. Paul sat in stunned silence for a while. He got up and poured himself a stiff drink, sculling it fast. He hoped the alcohol would assist in diluting flashbacks which had begun playing out in his mind.

His eyes became transfixed on the photo of Zac. He recalled how the silver photo frame shone in the sunlight catching his eye after he spent his first night in the arms of Michael. The embarrassment he felt when he picked it up and dropped in on the floor

173

breaking the glass. The glass still hadn't been replaced. Walking over and picking up the photo frame he looked deep into Zac's eyes.

The alcohol hadn't done its job; in fact, the reverse was happening. Memories began pouring out of his subconscious. The videos that were shown today of Zac and Dylan graduating. That face, almost the same as Michael's but not quite. He had seen that face before, Zac's face. The moles, the shape they formed, like a triangle.

'Where? Where was it? Why is it buried deep inside my mind?'

Becoming overwhelmed Paul put the photo back and sat down staring at it. Feeling anxious Paul began drawing shapes with his index finger on the top of his knee. This time he noticed what he was doing. He stared at his index finger drawing a shape; it had a life of its own. Drawing the same shape over and over again. The shape of a triangle.

The beep of the door opening broke the silence. Michael marched in taking the white plastic bags with tonight's dinner into the kitchen. "It's so cold and dark out there; it's just started raining too," Michael said trying to sound cheery.

He had felt a fracture in his relationship with Paul, but today the cracks had widened. Michael was grateful that Paul went to the memorial to support him; he'd hoped this would bring them closer together. It was an opportunity to reinforce the bond in their weakening relationship. The disconnect with Paul was still there today, there was no denying that.

The love Michael thought he had for Paul had well and truly gone.

"I need to speak with you," Paul said to Michael in a tone which had Michael worried.

Michael joined Paul on the sofa in the dimly lit room apart from the occasion bright flicker of the television. The men looked into each other's eyes. The colour had drained from Paul's face, Michael was growing concerned.

Paul blurted out, "It was me. I did it!"

Michael was confused, remaining silent.

"Zac. It was me! I did it! I murdered your brother!"

Michael leaned back on the sofa, his mind spinning, computing. Silence. Michael tried in vain to open his mouth. He couldn't. Numbness travelled from his head making its way right down to his toes. He was unable to move, almost comatose.

Paul began sobbing hysterically.

"I didn't know; I didn't know until today! Everything just came back to me now. His face, his face! Mikey, Mikey, say something!"

There was no response from Michael; he withdrew into himself, drowning in shock not believing what he was hearing.

Michael stood up. In a robotic motion, he marched to the bedroom. Emerging shortly after, wearing his favourite green running shorts with the reflective stripes. Showing no emotion, he proceeded to the door.

Paul ran to the door, standing in front of it, his arms spread open attempting to block Michael's exit. A stony-faced Michael reached under Paul's arms, picked him up, swinging his light body behind him and reached for the door handle. Paul jumped on his back, arms wrapped around his neck hysterically pleading for his boyfriend to stay.

Undeterred Michael opened the door, shook Paul off him, and walked out slamming the door. He stood outside the door for a moment wondering if he should march right back inside, grab Paul by the scruff of the neck and toss him out.

Unbeknown to Paul, Michael had already decided that tomorrow was the day he was going to have 'the talk' to Paul. By tomorrow night Paul won't be living with him any longer. Dylan would be on standby if the situation turned nasty.

In a state of shock at Paul's revelation, Michael was confused. *'Did Paul just say that he'd murdered Zac?'* It had been an emotionally exhausting day, buoyed by the impending extraction of Paul from his life tomorrow.

Back inside, Paul was on his knees sobbing uncontrollably. He wanted to explain he wasn't in his right mind, overcome with a cocktail of drugs when he repeatedly stabbed Zac to death. Paul didn't even know the guy. Occasionally, Paul would have vague flashbacks to that night. The moles on his victim's face in the shape of a triangle plagued his mind. He had no idea what it meant until he saw the video of Zac at the memorial.

Every detail of the horrendous drug-fuelled night came back to him. The blood splattered face. The painful cries from Zac each time the knife blade entered his body. Over and over until his victim, Zac, his boyfriend's brother, was silent. Paul had stumbled off into the night. The next morning, he woke up in a laneway in the city; a bloodied knife lay by his side. He couldn't remember the crime he'd committed but knew he had done someone some harm. Dried blood was on his hands and clothes. He buried the knife deep inside a rubbish bin and moved on.

Sometime after the murder, the police caught up with Paul. He was charged with embezzlement from his former employer. He stole money to pay for his partying lifestyle. A lifestyle involving heavy drug taking that caused his life to begin its descent into a hazy, disorganised ball of confusion. Paul was forced to attend drug and alcohol counselling, that's where he met Riley who became his counsellor.

Paul needed to find work as part of his rehab program. Riley had met Bob, the Pridemoores' gardener, a few times while visiting Julia at work. Explaining the situation to a sympathetic Bob, he agreed to take on Paul in his gardening business. Paul was able to be rehabilitated, eventually and proudly rebuilding a different and better life for himself. His family still refused to have anything to do with him; he wasn't particularly close with them anyway and could move on without them in his life.

Paul's life flashed through his mind; he had done well he thought, picked himself up and lived a fulfilled life. He felt himself slowly slipping back into some of his old ways. He began drinking alcohol and dabbling in drugs again after the influence of his old clubbing mate, Carro. The new life he had built could soon come crashing back down again.

Paul realised he could be doing some serious jail time if Michael told the police. Still, there was no proof. He'd gotten away with it so far, and it would only be his word against Michael's. Of course, he would deny he'd ever said it. However, he was certain Michael would tell Dylan, who wouldn't hesitrate to tell his copper boyfriend, Easton.

A switch flicked in Paul's mind. He untangled himself from the mangled ball of legs, arms and tears on the floor. Walking into the bedroom, he went to the wardrobe taking out a large black winter coat. He rummaged through a drawer searching for the black leather gloves and came across the trinkets he had stolen from Michael's parents' house. He laughed out loud.

"Perfect crime Paul," he whispered to himself. "Some people are so gullible. They all believed the old bastard had lost his marbles." He giggled. Dressed in Michael's black winter coat that was several sizes too large for him he left the apartment.

Standing on the footpath outside, he looked left and right; there was no sign of Michael. Paul knew where Michael would be running; he always runs the same route repeatedly.

It was late; no one was around. Paul walked along the wet footpath then rounded a corner. Noticing an older style car parked in the street, he had an idea. His former street smarts kicked in, without a second thought he broke into it. Opening the door, he was overcome with the smell of a half-eaten hamburger left on the driver's seat. He figured the owner of the car would be close by, so he needed to act fast. Hot-wiring a car came back to him all too easily, within seconds the engine started.

He drove the car to the vicinity of where he hoped to find Michael. Turning a corner, he drove slowly along a darkened street, large elm trees lining both sides of the road. He spotted a figure running along the footpath a few metres ahead. A reflective stripe illuminated from the headlights of the car. It was Michael.

Paul's heart galloped, he had to do this. Michael began to run across the road a short distance away. Calm and in control Paul planted his foot on the accelerator.

He steered the car directly towards his boyfriend. Michael looked right into Paul's eyes as he was flung over the bonnet of the car.

The force of being hit so hard sent Michael's large frame up in the air, landing against one of the large elm trees. His body lay half against the tree trunk and half in the gutter.

Paul sped off into the night.

DAVID GOLDON

EPILOGUE:
The Road Out Of Engle Byen

Six months later...

Paul shut the door to the apartment he shared with Michael. The elevator transported him to the car park. He sat in the driver's seat of the vehicle which was once the exclusive domain of Michael. Starting the engine, he drove the short distance to the hospital.

As he entered Michael's hospital room, Elaine and Ben were already there. Elaine was in hysterics; Ben tried as best he could to comfort her.

Shortly after, Julia and Riley arrived. Elaine and Ben were on one side of Michael's bed while Paul was on the other.

"Michael, it's mum, dad's here too. Paul, you go first."

"Mikey, I love you so much. We can't bear to let you live like this any longer. It's not living having all these wires and tubes keeping you alive; I know you would want to be set free, Mikey. It's been six months now, and nothing has changed; no improvement. If you can hear me, this is the saddest day of my life."

"Michael, dad and I agree with your boyfriend, Paul. We can't let you go on like this; you should be allowed to rest, my beautiful boy."

"Son know that we all love you dearly and this isn't a choice we made easily, we will miss you for the rest of our lives. Be free and fly my kind, beautiful son. We love you."

Dylan entered the room, cracks appearing in his professional façade. Aggressively nudging Paul out of the way, he stood at Michael's bedside next to the life support machine.

With tears rolling down her cheeks, Elaine nodded to Dylan.

Dylan placed one hand on Michael's chest. His other hand trembled as he reluctantly reached over and switched off the life support machine. Michael's chest ceased its rise and fall. Dylan's breathing quickened as a lump formed in his throat. He tried with every morsel of strength he had not to cry out loud. Fighting back a sea of tears his voice cracked as he managed to utter his last words to his best friend.

"Goodbye mate."

DAVID GOLDON

BONUS:

Two chapters from the upcoming book by

DAVID GOLDON

ENGLE BYEN
OPPORTUNITIES

Book three in the ENGLE BYEN series

DAVID GOLDON

CHAPTER ONE:

Glenda and Flo both worked at their local Opportunity Shop. Flo took advantage of every opportunity that came her way, while Glenda was a stickler for rules.

Glenda would always take the high road and do what was morally right with the 'opportunities' that crossed her path. 'Opportunities' could be in the form of cash found in pockets of clothing, expensive looking jewellery, high-end fashion and various brand-new items.

Cash was the most highly prized find when rummaging through the pockets of donated clothing. Pockets were always thoroughly checked before assessing the condition of a garment, pricing it and putting it out for sale.

Both women had been working at the Op Shop for several months; having nothing in common, they didn't see each other socially. Glenda had often suspected that Flo was taking any cash she found, slyly putting it in the front pocket of her apron.

When Glenda found cash in a pocket of clothing, she always held it up in the air and waved it about for all to see. The other ladies working in the backroom would applaud before Glenda dutifully handed it over to her manager. Flo very rarely found any cash, well any cash that she declared, which had raised suspicion from her co-workers, especially Glenda.

Glenda lives with her friend Melba in a modest home on the outskirts of a peaceful, idyllic country town called Random. Random can only be accessed from a bypass off the main highway. In years gone by, before the bypass was built, Random boasted a bustling town centre due to the many tourists that would stop by on their way through to other destinations.

Glenda's parents had long since passed; she'd never lived anywhere else other than the house she was raised in. Both women were content and enjoyed each other's company, except for the occasional tiff.

Melba works at the local haberdashery store. She is in her element being surrounded by beautiful fabrics, often bringing home new curtains for the house. Melba's obsession with constantly changing curtains was a source of friction between the two, which didn't deter Melba in the slightest.

Glenda was more practical when it came to such things; she thought it was a waste for Melba to be buying new curtains when the curtains they had were still as perfect as the day they were hung. Glenda would gather Melba's off casts, be it clothes, bric-a-brac or curtains and donate them to the Op Shop.

Glenda has always been a saver and living with her parents she only paid a minimal amount of board as they had requested. She had been working in the administration department at the local council all her life, up to a few months ago, when she was made redundant.

Looking every one of her fifty-eight years, she still maintained her lean figure by walking most days and steering clear of fatty foods. Grey haired and proud of it, she didn't care too much about other people's thoughts of her; she marched to the beat of her own drum.

Her friends admired her courage at not wanting to be like everyone else, while it irritated others immensely. Her dry sense of humour would either make you laugh or scratch your head wondering if she was insulting you.

The rotund, big bosomed, heavily perfumed with lavender talc Flo, put on her latex gloves ready for another day of sorting through clothes that had been donated to the Op Shop. It was like trash and treasure for her, depending if there was any treasure to be found. Three large cardboard boxes filled most of the space out the back of the shop.

Flo was alone at the time waiting for the other ladies to arrive. There was no way she was going to begin to tackle those boxes alone, so she removed her gloves in favour of making herself a cup of tea. She sat for about five minutes daydreaming, waking up when she heard the tinkle of the bell attached to the front door. Glenda walked the short distance through the shop to the backroom.

"Good morning, Flo," she cheerfully chirped.

"Morning, Glen," came the morose reply.

"What's wrong with you dear?" a concerned Glenda asked.

Flo motioned her hand over to the boxes as she sighed, "Looks like it's going to be a busy day."

Glenda joined Flo for a cuppa; they were chatting away until they heard the tinkle of the bell above the shop door. Irma, the store manager, had arrived.

"Morning, Ladies!" Irma yelled across the shop.

"Morning, Irma!" Flo and Glenda yelled back in unison.

"Nice to see she decided to turn up for work today," Flo whispered to Glenda.

Irma would often call in sick much to Flo's annoyance, meaning extra work for Flo who was second in charge of the store.

Irma began organising the shop for the day ahead, putting the cash into the register, wiping down the glass cabinets which housed small ornaments and bits'n'pieces.

Glenda and Flo slipped on their latex gloves ready for a day of sorting through the donated clothes and whatever else was contained in the three large cardboard boxes in the backroom. They selected a box each and pushed it along the concrete floor to their respective workbenches.

Reaching into the box, Glenda took out a garment, checked through the pockets, inspected it for wear and tear and placed it in the spot where it would be later priced and placed out for sale. She was like a machine once she got going.

Flo, on the other hand, would just take her time, she figured there was no hurry why push herself. After taking out the third garment for inspection, Flo's eyes lit up behind her fancy pink-framed glasses at the sight of a designer blouse with the tags still attached. Glancing over at Glenda working away opposite her, she folded it up and put in back in the box. She would wait until Glenda was on a break, retrieve the blouse and smuggle it out of the shop with her tonight.

Flo couldn't believe the amount of good quality designer label clothing she was unearthing. She knew she couldn't smuggle it all out of the store without being detected and there was nowhere she could stash it away for another day. She thought perhaps she should follow the rules; let the garments go into the shop for seven days before staff were allowed to purchase it. This stuff wouldn't last for seven days in the shop, the so-called serial treasure hunters that trawled Op Shops in search of high quality, low priced merchandise would pounce on these items in the blink of an eye.

Flo wished she had some friends that she could send into the shop and purchase items for her, but no way would she admit to anyone that she worked in an Op Shop, let alone would wear clothes from an Op Shop.

Being on a meagre income and having a taste for the high life didn't go hand in hand. Keeping up appearances meant everything to her. She always heavily dosed herself with lavender talcum powder before arriving for work, fearful she would leave smelling like mothballs.

Flo had lived very comfortably all her life, never short of money and always immaculately presented until of course; her deadbeat former husband took it all away from her. She earned a meagre amount of income from working at the shop, which didn't stretch far enough. It was only ever from the Op Shop she would steal to make ends meet. No harm done, no one would miss anything, was how she justified her unspeakable behaviour as a petty thief.

"Do you need a hand there dear?" Glenda asked.

"No, fine thanks, love," Flo responded.

"I've finished this box, some nice stuff in there we can get some good money for them; the charity will be pleased. Such lovely people donating things we can actually sell instead of all the usual rubbish we have to throw out. Anyway, it's nearly 10 o'clock, cuppa tea and bickie time. You coming?" Glenda said as she walked away from her station to the small makeshift tea room.

"Be there in a jiff dear!" Flo yelled out.

Now she was faced with a dilemma, with Glenda out of the way for a while it was time to make her move, but what would she take first? She didn't bring a big shopping bag with her today, so it could only be one item. She reached into the box and took out the blouse, looking around the backroom as she folded it up and put in under her apron. Slowly making her way to her locker, she opened it, had another quick glance around the room, stuffed the blouse into the locker and shut it.

"Well, are you coming?" Glenda shouted out causing Flo a near cardiac arrest.

CHAPTER TWO:

Tuesday's were generally a quiet day in the shop which Irma utilised to remove the dead flies from the front window and replace the stock. She would be there for hours umming and erring about where and how to place the lace doilies, crocheted blankets, tired looking teddy bears and cross-eyed dolls.

She fancied herself as a stylist after watching all those reality shows on TV; she was better than any of the contestants on those shows, she thought. Her constant redecorating at home was a bugbear for her husband, he was often asked to paint the interior walls of their house to whatever the latest colour trend was.

Irma would forage through ornaments and trinkets donated to the store in search of items she could purchase and take home, after all, everything old is new again.

Walking out onto the footpath she stood near the kerb looking at the shop. She admired the two windows she had just dressed, *'Yes perfect,'* she thought.

The front door, which separated the two windows, was covered in fingerprints; that will never do. Irma marched inside the store and went behind the counter to get some window cleaner and newspaper to wipe the door window with. She placed the newspaper on the shop counter and opened it up to take a few pages out. *'Oh, that's interesting,'* she thought, as she noticed a headline that caught her eye: 'Holland Mansion Robbed'.

Holland Mansion was a huge house on top of Squires Hill which looked down upon the town. The mansion was surrounded by a border of eucalypt trees, a lowly stacked limestone brick wall just behind the trees led up steep steps to the front wrap around veranda. All the locals knew about the mansion but not the mysterious and reclusive Holland's.

The family had made their fortune in eco trading, not that any of the locals understood what exactly eco trading was, not being related to farming. The family didn't like to make a fuss about themselves, often donating to local charities and supporting their local community as anonymously as possible; which can prove difficult in a small town. The Holland's were new money, their home was purpose-built utilising all the latest eco-friendly technology and had featured in many magazines and television shows.

Irma continued to read the article. The Holland family were moving some items into their home when the removalist's truck was stolen from the front of their home. It was driven away too fast for the removalist to see who was driving it. The truck contained at least three large cardboard boxes full of various items, the contents yet to be ascertained by the family.

Irma's concentration was interrupted when she heard the ladies bickering out back. She left the front counter to investigate the kerfuffle.

"Ladies, ladies, please keep the noise down, I can hear you arguing from out the front!" she said with a tone of assertion to Glenda and Flo.

"How much do you reckon for this picture?" Flo asked Irma holding up a stretched canvas print for her to see.

"Well," Irma hesitated, eyeballing the rather ugly painting, "Forty dollars, I guess."

"Glenda here, who obviously has no artistic bones in her old body, was going to mark it twenty dollars."

"It's ugly; no one would want that, I could do better," Glenda laughed, "Who's Andy Warhol anyway?"

"Well, it may not be an original, but I'm sure there are some artistic types, like myself, that would appreciate it," Flo huffed back.

'Hmmm,' Glenda thought, maybe she could buy it for Melba's upcoming birthday.

The tinkle of the bell over the shop door rang as the ladies stopped gossiping and turned to look at the visitor. Noticing it was a police officer, all three ladies quickly left the back-room eager to find out what he wanted.

Hearts began fluttering and cheeks turned a shade of rose as the handsome officer made his way to the front counter. He was tall, well built, handsomely rugged with tanned olive skin. His emerald green eyes glistened as he looked each lady in the eyes. He smiled a perfect pearl white smile, causing the ladies hearts to thump faster; even Glenda's.

Nonchalantly, Glenda broke the silence, "Can I help you, officer?"

"Sergeant actually, Sergeant Easton Barlow," his deep, gravelly voice replied.

"Sergeant Barlow, I'm Flo, this is Irma, and this is Glenda," Flo cooed waving her hand at her work colleagues while introducing them.

A flirtatious Irma pushed in front of Glenda and Flo, "I'm the store manager, Sergeant Barlow, let me show you around my shop. Are you looking for something for your wife?"

Glenda turned to Flo rolling her eyes.

"No, I'm not married, and you can call me Easton," he smiled, almost laughing out aloud. Flo nudged and winked at Glenda who returned serve with an unimpressed, indifferent expression on her face.

"I'm sure we have something here for your little lady friend then." Irma pirouetted, holding her arms in the air like a twelve-year-old ballerina.

Easton let out a girlish giggle. "Sorry Irma, my partner wouldn't be pleased if I bought *him* some of the lovely doilies you have in the front window."

A rather deflated Irma replied, "It's not all doilies you know, look around. What does your, uummm, partner do for a living?"

"He's a doctor in the city, that's where I'm from as well. I'm just here in Ransom for a few months filling in for your local sergeant who's on extended leave."

"Oh, a doctor? You lucky man you," Flo cooed as Glenda's face remained stoic, "You should have brought him along with you dear."

"He's in a bad place at the moment; his best friend's in a coma. He was involved in a hit and run while he was out jogging one night," a forlorn Easton explained, "I feel bad being away from him, but he insisted I take up this job here, it's only for a few months."

A sympathetic Glenda chimed in, "I'm so sorry to hear that, I lost both of my parents in a car accident many years ago, so tragic."

"Thanks ladies, I appreciate your concern. I'm not here for shopping; I'm actually here on official police business."

All the women gasped. Flo's heart rate increased, were they onto her? Surely not, they can't be; it was only a few bits'n'bobs she took home without paying, every now and then. Well, nearly every shift she worked actually. She was filled with dread, was her little gig up? Would this handsome sergeant throw the cuffs on her and toss her in the back of his divvy van? She would never be able to show her face in town again. Maybe after her long stint in prison, no one in town would remember her?

"Sergeant Barlow, we are a reputable boutique, everything is above board I can assure you," Irma responded with an air of grace, "Isn't that right ladies? These girls have been working with me for months, sergeant; I can personally vouch for them. Unless, of course, they have committed any heinous crimes prior to that."

Flo's cheeks changed colour.

Unimpressed by Irma's backhanded compliment Glenda joined the conversation, "That's right, and no matter what crime Irma may have committed, I would stand by her as well."

"Ladies, Ladies! None of you have committed any crimes, well none that I know of," Sergeant Barlow smiled, "Are you aware that a removalist van was stolen from the Holland Mansion? It contained some valuable items. The van was recovered a couple of kilometres away, but it was empty. Sometimes crooks fence stolen property in junk shops like this."

A horrified Irma let out an audible gasp. Sergeant Barlow quickly corrected himself, "I mean, high-end boutiques retailing in pre-loved merchandise, like your establishment here." Irma was pleasantly impressed at the sergeant's correction.

Stony-faced Glenda remained unimpressed, arms crossed, glaring at the pair. Sensing it was time he left the store Easton Barlow cheerily said, "I'll come back with a list of the missing items and possibly some photos that the Holland family are compiling. Good day, ladies." He turned and quickly strode out of the store before the women could engage him in any further conversation.

"Gays in the police force, what's the world coming to?" Flo gasped.

"It's not 1950 anymore Flo, get with the times. Gays and lesbians can even get married!" an annoyed Glenda replied harshly.

"Well, hopefully none in this town, heaven forbid." Flo retorted.

DAVID GOLDON

Coming soon
from
DAVID GOLDON

ENGLE BYEN
OPPORTUNITIES

Book three in the ENGLE BYEN series

www.DavidGoldon.com

The Road To ENGLE BYEN

DAVID GOLDON

About the Author

David attended a newly formed writing group to support his friends. He had no intention, patience or time to write any stories himself, or so he thought. Inadvertently he was drawn into participating in some writing exercises. His long-cobwebbed creativity began to emerge transitioning into a new-found passion for story writing. David aims to infiltrate the LGBT literary world with stories of love, life and lessons learned with an Australian flavour.

David lives in Melbourne, Australia with his long-term partner and two fur babies.

www.DavidGoldon.com

DAVID GOLDON

About Ava Orion Media

DAVID GOLDON

*Have you ever dreamt of holding your own published book
in your hands?*

AVA ORION Media
can make that self-publishing dream come true!

We also help with smaller work like written content for
websites, blogs, essays and so forth. If you're finding it
challenging to determine the appropriate spelling, grammar
or how to effectively express what you want to say... we
would love to help you!

So email: info@AvaOrionMedia.com now!

~

I never had bedtime stories read to me as a child.
I never read books as a child, but some things are meant to be
some passions are in our DNA,
they travel with us through lifetimes
and nothing can hold them down.
So now I love to read, more than that, I LOVE proofreading,
editing and writing.
I would love to read your stories, that's always an exciting
adventure for me, and then I'll help you put your best words
forward...

Michael Young
Founder ~ Ava Orion Media

I believe in the power of our words.

www.AvaOrionMedia.com
www.MichaelYoungAuthor.com

▶ YouTube *Search:* Ava Orion Media

213

DAVID GOLDON

DAVID GOLDON